OTHER BOOKS BY LORIN GRACE

Hastings 2
SECURITY

THE Not BODYGUARD'S Widow

LORIN GRACE

CURRANT
CREEK PRESS

Cover Design © 2019 Evan Frederickson and LJP Creative Graphics
Photos © iStock

Formatting by LJP Creative
Edits by Eschler Editing

Published by Currant Creek Press
North Logan, Utah
Not the Bodyguard's Widow© 2020 by Lorin Grace

First edition: March 2020
ISBN: 978-1-970148-05-3

to Cami

SHALL WE GO FOR A WALK?

CANDLE WAX DRIPPED ONTO GRANDMOTHER'S embroidered
linen tablecloth. Kimberly pushed her chair back from the end
of the table and blew out each flickering flame, then listened as
the grandfather clock in the entrance hall played "Lord Bless
This Hour" before chiming the first of ten counts. Flipping on
the lights, she groaned. More wax speckled the tablecloth than
what she'd seen running from the greedy little flames, the candle
nearest her husband's vacant seat having left a small ring. Letting
the candles burn for hours was a mistake. She'd lost track of time
staring into the dancing lights, knowing that Jeremy would enter
the house any moment. At least she'd chosen the white candles,
rather than red, for Valentine's Day or the pink and blue ones to
hint at her surprise. She'd google how to remove the wax from
the heirloom.

In the kitchen, Kimberly turned the oven from warm to off,
then grabbed a roll and smeared it with raspberry jam. The dinner
she'd prepared no longer whetted her appetite, but she knew
better than to go to bed on an empty stomach. A wedge of the
Edam cheese balanced the carbs she consumed. Her view from
the kitchen window blurred as tears filled her eyes.

Kimberly stored the entire pan of Chicken Cacciatore in the refrigerator. She wouldn't touch it, but the bodyguards Jeremy insisted keep watch over her would. Over the last five years, she'd mastered eluding them. She owed today's disappearance to her OB-GYN appointment. They didn't deserve to know the news before her husband did, and so she'd ditched them by walking out the backdoor of the restaurant. Her bodyguards had learned about her last two miscarriages before Jeremy had, and they'd reported them to her father-in-law before she could call her husband. She berated herself for the umpteenth time. Why did she continue to believe Jeremy's lies? The five-thirty text reassuring her he would be home in a half hour was the latest of five years of falsehoods. It would have been easier had he been covering up an affair.

On their Thanksgiving cruise, he'd promised to make things right at work, even if it meant paying a hefty fine. His promises of putting her first were believable under the Caribbean sun, but after their return, his late nights grew later and later as he *supposedly* met with the FBI, SEC, IRS, or some other government alphabet-soup agency only to come home smelling of his father's cigars and causing her to wonder if he had been honest about the Ponzi scheme the company ran. Her Christmas present of $10,000 cash to hold her over "just in case" should have warned her that the lies hadn't stopped. And he'd grown even more secretive in the last seven weeks. Why wasn't he the man she thought she'd married?

Perhaps she should march into the FBI and explain what little she knew. Which was nothing. The conversations had ended when she'd entered the room and Jeremy insisted that what they had done couldn't really be considered a Ponzi scheme and would not impress any agents. What would it mean for the child growing inside her to have a criminal for a father?

Kimberly cleared the fruit bowl from the table. According to the expectant-mom website, her little he or she was the size of a navel orange this week. Oranges didn't pair well with the rest of the dinner menu. She'd put them on the table mostly so they could talk about what the beginning of their second trimester meant.

The love of money *was* the root of all evil. The biblical statement had proven true in her marriage. She would have been better off marrying a poor plaid-wearing man like the heroes in all those Hearthfire Christmas movies. A desire to rage and scream filled her, but she knew that even though she'd dismissed the staff for the evening, she was likely being watched.

If only she could be a starving artist again. But even her career, which Jeremy referred to as a hobby, had gone too far for that. Her illustrated children's books were now in demand. If he had any idea exactly how much she made, she'd never get her father-in-law out of her life, not until he had it invested in his firm.

The grandfather clock chimed half past the hour. Kimberly turned off the downstairs lights and checked the alarm panel, inputting the code showing she was in the house alone and retiring for the night. Halfway up the stairs, the alarm beeped, indicating security had allowed a car past the front gate. The alarm wouldn't have sounded for Jeremy's car. Kimberly turned and hurried down the stairs.

Jax, one of the bodyguards, met her in the entryway, having let himself in the house. "It's a police car, ma'am. Would you like to talk to them on the porch or in the sitting room?"

Apparently it was a forgone conclusion that she would talk with the police. She chose an option Jax hadn't given her and stepped between the large guard and the double doors. "I'll answer the door."

On the steps stood a young officer and her older partner, hats in hand. "Mrs. Kimberly Thompson?"

"That is me."

"We are here to inform you that your husband was in a drunk-driving accident on Shoreline Road, about fifty miles north of here."

"Who hit him? Which hospital is he at?" She could forgive him for being late since it wasn't his fault. Fifty miles? Why Oregon? Jeremy had been coming home. She reached for the wall to steady herself. She should have eaten more.

The older officer shook his head. "No one else was involved, ma'am. I am sorry to inform you—your husband is dead."

No! They were wrong. Jeremy never drank more than a glass of wine and then only on rare occasions. "But he doesn't dri—" The officers' faces faded as oblivion enveloped her.

Three Months Later

THURSDAY MORNINGS WERE THE QUIETEST of the week. Alex read through the security reports from the various C&O holdings entrusted to Hastings Security. Last night's violent Northern Indiana thunderstorm had toppled a tree at the Crawfords's property and caused a power outage and alarm failure at Candace Ogilvie's Art House. The local contract security company had determined in a drive-by that a downed limb on the roof was causing the skylight alarm to go off every twenty minutes ever since the power had come back on this morning. The limb had been removed, but the alarm continued to send out false alerts. The system was proprietary to Hastings Security, and the security contractor didn't have the parts to make a repair.

A deliberate ploy on Hastings's part. Several of the college students who roomed together at Art House had not only embarked on successful careers but married six of the wealthiest men in the country. Since the women had painted almost every available surface in the house during their Friday-night pizza parties, the walls, cupboards, and doors were now worth hundreds of thousands of dollars. The fewer people who knew about the interior, the better. Candace Ogilvie had yet to decide what to do with her old house since her marriage, and so it remained alarmed and maintained.

Many of the Hastings Security employees had been assigned for events related to the Mother's Day weekend, but with the Crawfords and Ogilvies in Europe for an extended vacation, he wasn't likely to get any calls from them.

Alex crossed the hall to his father's office. "Do you mind if I run down to C&O's Indiana properties? There was storm damage at the cottage, and the Art House alarm system is sounding false signals every twenty minutes. The local service has messaged me seven times this morning."

Jethro Hastings swiped through several screens on his tablet. "Sure you don't want to send someone else? Anyone on Alan's tech crew can fix a faulty alarm. Sounds like a classic case of something going bump in the night and nothing to worry about."

"I would like to get away from the office for a bit." And the family. With his twin sister expecting triplets and his older brother practically engaged to the mother of a six-month-old, Alex wanted some time away from the craziness. Baby things everywhere and Mom looking at him and the rest of the brothers as if wondering when they would find wives.

His father studied him for a long moment. "Take an extra day. We have things covered here. Be back in time for Sunday dinner. Your mother wants everyone together for Mother's Day."

Alex turned to leave.

"And, son, on that extra day off, hike, fish, or do something for you. Don't turn it into a working vacation day."

Alex didn't bother dropping by his condo as he left town. His go-bag was packed with enough clothing for three days, and he had a full week of clothes at the old caretaker's house on the Crawford property, which Hastings's bodyguards used as a base when the Crawfords or Ogilvies vacationed in Indiana. The repair on the alarm wouldn't take more than an hour, and if there had been a break-in, Candace's nosy neighbor would have called 911. Candace's roommate had been correct the day they installed the security system—the sleepy college town didn't have enough crime to worry about. And with neighbors like Candace's, the system was redundant.

The traffic thinned as he drove deeper into Indiana, and soon he found himself on a two-lane highway surrounded alternately by trees and farms and freshly plowed fields. Yellow warning signs cautioned drivers to slow down for buggies and reminded Alex he had yet to visit the Shipshewana Menno-Hof information center, which detailed the history of the Amish and Mennonites in the area. He could look at the Amish furniture store to find Mom a unique gift for Mother's Day. He turned his head to tell his sister his thoughts only to find an empty seat. How often had he done that in the past year? Once or twice a day at least.

Houses soon replaced farms, scattered leaves and branches littering the lawns and driveways of the Art House and other residences on the quiet street.

Before going in, Alex walked the perimeter, assessing the damage. A few twigs lay on the roof, but nothing big enough to trigger an alarm malfunction. A paver near the side door to the garage lay askew. He picked it up and found a small box-shaped indentation in the soil. Alex inspected the door. Three muddy fingerprints. They had not been there three weeks ago when the Ogilvies had come down for Easter. And last night's storm would have washed away anything old. Candace knew better than to leave a key buried outside. Alex searched around the house again. A small footprint in the soft earth near the AC unit raised more suspicions. Maybe the alarm wasn't a malfunction.

Alex pulled out his phone and called Alan, the automated system routing his call to Hastings's reception desk.

"Hey, Elle, it's Alex. Alan didn't answer. Is he out of the office?"

"No, Mr. Alexander. Mr. Alan is meeting with Mr. Hastings," Elle answered, using their business names. With three brothers and his father working at the firm, calling them all Mr. Hastings was confusing.

"Will you see if they'll take my call?"

"Yes, Mr. Alexander." The line went silent for a moment, then Elle's voice came back on the line. "There is a DND code on the meeting. Do you want me to interrupt?"

Do not disturb. His father didn't use it often. "No, I'll call back if I need them." A single small-footed intruder couldn't be that much trouble. If they had broken in. Alex brought up the Hastings Security app on his phone and tapped in his code, then remotely disabled the alarm to the side door and the door from the garage to the kitchen. Next, he sent a quick text to the local security contractor, telling them he was on-site.

Alex opened the door and drew his gun. If someone had disassembled the house and sold Candace's stuff on eBay, it would devastate her.

He entered the house noiselessly. A half-filled cup of lukewarm peppermint tea— assuming the discarded wrapper was correct— sat on the table. A single bowl sat in the draining rack next to the sink. How had someone gotten in and stayed in without setting off the alarms? The question could wait until he found the intruder.

Alex worked quickly to clear the rooms. His favorite murals remained untouched. In the back bedroom, the one his sister Abbie had used when she'd worked here last year, the bed was only half made. A suitcase stood by the closet door. A squatter.

Nothing was out of place in the library other than a book or two from the second case where the dust was disturbed. None of the books was worth more than the price printed above the barcode. Alex circled the base of the spiral staircase that led to the loft above the library before climbing up. There was no way to enter the second-floor room carefully. It was headfirst or nothing.

Halfway up the stairs he heard a female voice ring out. "Stop! Drop your gun, or I'll shoot!"

KIMBERLY KNELT BETWEEN THE BEANBAGS, struggling to keep her hands steady. The oversize plush bag in front of her wasn't much of a protective barrier. The blond-haired man looked like he had fallen out of one of those CIA-based movies. But good looks didn't mean he was a good guy. How had they found her so fast?

She held her hands steady as she could. "I said to drop the gun."

The man's deep-blue eyes studied her for a moment before he raised his left hand above his head, his gun flat on the palm of his right.

"I said to drop it." *Please, please drop it.* She'd never fired a gun before.

The man did something with his gun, making it click, then set two parts on the floor next to him. In the process, he came up another step, revealing part of his torso. The logo on his shirt claimed he was with Hastings Security.

"What are you doing here?" This time she held the gun steady.

"I'm Mr. Alexander of Hastings Security. And I should ask you the same thing."

"I'm not trespassing. The owner gave me a key." Eight years ago, and it no longer fit in the locks.

"But it didn't work, did it?"

How did he know? "I'm in, aren't I?"

Mr. Alexander rose another step, his waist now visible. Definitely one of the drop-dead gorgeous Michelangelo sculptured bodyguards Candace had described the day Kimberly complained about hers. "Stay back or I'll shoot."

He shook his head. "I don't think so. If you wanted to kill me, you would have blown my head off the moment you saw my hair."

It would be a shame to ruin his sandy-blond hair. What was she thinking? Pregnancy hormones. She needed to be brave for the baby. She'd eluded her father-in-law's goons. She could shoot him if he came closer, and then she'd run again.

He took another step, and Kimberly simultaneously squeezed the trigger and shut her eyes, but there was only a tiny pop.

Before she knew what was happening, he'd wrenched the gun from her hand, grabbed her wrist, and was pushing her onto the beanbag's soft fabric with his weight.

Kimberly screamed.

He rolled off her but kept her wrists in his hand. Kimberly tried to jerk away.

The man gasped and dropped her hands. "Did I hurt you or the baby?"

Her hands flew to her belly to protect her child as she shook her head.

"I'm sorry. I didn't notice before. I wouldn't have tackled you." He sat on the balls of his feet between her and the stairway, like a leopard ready to spring. "Now, what are you doing here?"

"Why didn't the gun go off?"

"It did."

"I missed?"

"You shouldn't shut your eyes when you shoot. Let me repeat. What are you doing here?"

"I, um," Kimberly said. "I'm a guest." It was close enough. Candace said she could visit anytime. The slight fact she hadn't spoken to Candace since Candace had married Collin Ogilvie last New Year's Eve might be a problem.

"I see. And does Candace know you are here?"

Kimberly bit her lip. "I've been trying to call her for three days, but all my calls go to voicemail. I've had her number memorized for years. I know I have been dialing it correctly."

"Where have you been calling from?"

"I tried a pay phone and my new cell." Kimberly held up the burner phone.

"You say you know Candace?"

Kimberly nodded.

"May I try to call her?" He held out his hand.

Kimberly clutched her phone to her chest "No. I am never supposed to share her number."

Mr. Alexander smiled and relaxed as he lifted his own phone and initiated a video call.

Candace's voice soon filled the small loft. "Alex? What's wrong?"

"Can you identify this woman for me?" Mr. Alexander turned the phone to face Kimberly, Candace's face and bright-blue hair filling the screen.

"Kimberly? Is that Lover's Loft? What are you two doing there?"

Mr. Alexander turned the phone back to him. "I'm not sure yet. Does she have permission to stay at Art House?"

"I told her she was always welcome. How did she get in? Kimberly, did you come through the skylight again? If you broke the skylight this time..."

"I didn't break it." Kimberly crossed her arms.

Mr. Alexander glanced from the skylight to Kimberly's baby bump and back. "Don't worry, Mrs. Ogilvie. I'll take care of things."

"Alex, don't you Mrs. Ogilvie me. Let me talk to Kimberly."

Mr. Alexander handed Kimberly the phone.

"What is going on? I got a frantic call yesterday, I mean late Tuesday, from your phone—a man claiming to be your father-in-law saying you need to contact him."

Kimberly felt behind her for the wall. "My phone? I destroyed my phone Monday. This was a bad idea. I'm sorry, Candace. I'll go someplace else. Please don't tell him you know where I am."

Candace wrinkled her painted-on brows. "He said you left the hospital and that you'd had a miscarriage and might be suicidal."

"Yes, I left the hospital, but I faked the miscarriage." She moved the phone to show Candace her baby bump, stretching the T-shirt tight over her belly. "And I am not suicidal, but if he finds me, he will make it look like I took my life. Jeremy's father wants me gone for good."

"Kimberly!"

"Can I explain later?" Not in front of this Mr. Alexander. Candace was normally a good judge of character. She'd warned her Jeremy wasn't the right man five years ago, but just because Candace trusted her bodyguard didn't mean Kimberly had to.

Mr. Alexander listened to every word with his arms crossed, his presence filling the small loft.

"We'll catch up when I am back in the States. Don't run away. And trust Alex. He is the best."

"Thanks, Candace." She looked at the guard. He was definitely confident, but that didn't equate to trustworthy.

"Oh, before we go, I want to see baby bump again. I am so glad you didn't have another miscarriage."

Kimberly held the phone out so she could fit her upper body on the screen.

"Oh, so cute! Do you know what flavor?"

"I asked them not to tell me."

"How far along are you?"

"Twenty-five weeks."

"Mandy has a doctor in Chicago she loves. She didn't trust the ones down near the house. I'll tell you all about her later." Candace turned her head. "I gotta go. Trust Alex. He is as good as he looks!" The call ended.

Kimberly handed the phone back.

Mr. Alexander was a shade pinker around his ears. "Did you really come through the skylight?"

Kimberly nodded. "I took a chance it might not be alarmed or with the power outage it wouldn't report. I guess it did."

"Every twenty minutes since the power came back on. I think it reported initially, but because of the lightning strike at the substation, our local contractor missed it as their power went out too." Mr. Alexander stood, crouching under the loft's sloped ceiling, and inspected the skylight. He pulled out his phone. "I'm disabling this link for a few moments." He opened the window and closed it again, then looked at his phone. "Was it raining when you came in last night?"

"Yes."

"Did you reconnect the alarm ends?"

"Yes. It is similar to the system my father-in-law installed at our house."

He looked at her for a moment before turning back to the alarm connector. "The connector must have gotten wet. There was enough humidity to cause it to signal an alarm every twenty minutes."

"So if it hadn't been raining, I wouldn't have set it off?" A raindrop had given her away?

"You set it off when you came in. But with half the county without power, they missed the initial alarm. If it had only been the one time, I would have asked the locals to investigate. However, they can't fix a broken alarm sensor. This system is proprietary, and we don't give them parts to fix anything that breaks, so I came down assuming it needed a repair."

"It must have been inconvenient to drive all the way from Chicago."

"Not really. Never happened before. I need to let my brother Alan know about this. Rarely does a sensor get wet, but it could happen again." He stepped back from the window and tapped his phone screen. "There, fixed. Let's go downstairs, and you can tell me what you didn't tell Candace." He held out a hand.

Kimberly rolled out of the beanbag chair and onto all fours, then stood without his help. Mr. Alexander dropped his hand, scooped up the guns, and descended the stairs.

She waited until he was out of sight, then rubbed her belly. "Candace trusts him. Can we?"

Alex put his gun back together, then fastened it into his holster. He studied the practice gun he'd taken from Kimberly. Candace must have left it here after one of her self-defense lessons. Good thing he'd found Kimberly and not the local security team. They might not have realized they were not in danger and taken the first shot. Coincidence or divine intervention? Alex assumed the latter. They could have ruined three lives with a real bullet.

"You never told me why the gun didn't shoot right." Kimberly watched him from halfway down the spiral staircase.

He lifted the gun, aimed at a vase on the table, and pulled the trigger. A red laser beam shot out, accompanied by a pop. "It is one of Hastings's training guns. Same weight and recoil as a real gun, but no damage."

"So I laser-tagged you."

"If you hadn't missed, you would have."

"Then why did you tackle me if you knew it wasn't real?"

He rubbed the side of the gun. "I wasn't positive it was ours until you shot it. I was already in motion."

"Oh." Kimberly reached the bottom of the stairs. "Can we talk in the kitchen? I was about to make myself some lunch when you pulled up."

In the kitchen, she opened several cupboards and the freezer. "Sorry, it doesn't look like I have more than the single bag of food I purchased last night at the convenience store. There are some old fish sticks and spices." She reached in the back of the cupboard. "Oh, and a brownie mix—but no eggs."

"Don't worry about me." Alex took a seat at the table.

After filling two glasses with water and setting them on the table, Kimberly pulled out a small quarter of cheese, a bag of baby carrots, and a bagel and placed them on a plate. Alex made a mental note to check the food situation before he left.

"Don't look at my plate that way." Kimberly sat across from him.

"What way?"

"Like you wonder how I will survive." She bit into a carrot.

"I was going to make sure you had more groceries." Didn't pregnant women eat for two? No wonder she hardly showed at more than halfway through her pregnancy. His frame of reference could be off, though. One baby took up less room than the three his sister Abbie was expecting.

"I'd planned on going out today until I realized leaving would set off the alarm system. I found some emergency food in the tornado shelter and figured I had enough nutrients for a week. If I didn't reach Candace by then, I was going to risk calling her husband's office." She broke off part of the bagel.

Alex leaned back, hoping his relaxed posture would help set Kimberly at ease. "You are an unknown or, rather, an uncleared caller. As long as you refuse to leave a voicemail, the network will block your call. Candace never even sees the unknown-caller calls."

"Oh, that explains it. This is my second burner. I dumped the last one when I landed in Indianapolis."

"I gather you are hiding from your father-in-law and you believe your life is in danger. Will you fill me in on the rest?"

Kimberly stiffened and stuck a carrot in her mouth.

Wrong tactic. He tried another route. "Why don't I tell you about me while you're eating?"

The question garnered a single nod.

"As I told you, my name is Mr. Alexander, but my friends know me as Alex Hastings. Candace calls me by my first name because we were friends first ..." There wasn't a good way to explain.

Anyone who knew Candace well would know she didn't put up with stuffiness for long.

"And she is Candace."

"The reason I go by Mr. Alexander is my brothers and I all work for our father at Hastings Security. Five "Mr. Hastings" got confusing fast, so my father is Mr. Hastings, then there are Mr. Adam, Mr. Alan, Mr. Andrew, and me. When my sister, Abbie, worked with us, she was Miss Hastings."

Kimberly turned the bagel over and over.

Alex waved at her plate. "Keep eating. Yes, my mother regrets all A names now and blames it on pregnancy brain. And the boys are alphabetical by age. I think Mom planned on more girls so she started out with Abigail. My sister is expecting triplets, and not only has she sworn not to name them with rhyming names, she has promised no alliteration or A names. The four of us would threaten her husband to make sure it sticks, but that would cause other problems as he is Preston Harmon."

Kimberly's eyes widened. "Your sister is the bodyguard who married the media mogul? Is that working for her? Please tell me she didn't marry for money."

"I have photos." Alex opened his photo gallery. "She seems thrilled to be with him, and they are so over-the-top in love it's sickening. Money was actually not in his favor. Like any body-guard, Abbie has seen the problems that come with it." He swiped past a photo the day of the impromptu baby shower and another from last Sunday's family dinner. There were several more of her showing off her times-three baby bump.

"She looks happy. You are sure it's real?"

The comment wasn't what he expected.

"Abbie is my twin. I know her real smile." Alex took the phone back and found a photo of Abbie on a hang-gliding trip they'd taken together before starting work for their father. "See? That is a genuine smile." He flipped to a photo of her senior year of high school. "This is the night all four of us took her to prom after running her date off. That is a very fake smile. Preston compliments her life in a way I can't understand. He's even convinced her to stop carrying her gun during the pregnancy. Even Mom couldn't do that." Alex flipped through his photos. "And here is a diabolical smile." He showed her the photo of their Halloween costumes when they were twelve.

"The wonder twins?"

"One of her friends dared her to get me to wear a unitard for Halloween. She tricked me into doing a twin theme, claiming it would be the last year we could dress up since we were twelve. Somehow I even suggested the wonder twins."

Kimberly covered her mouth as she laughed. "Who is the space monkey?"

"Andrew, my youngest brother. I have no idea how she got him to dress up as a purple monkey." Alex swiped to another photo from the same night.

Tears formed at the corners of Kimberly's eyes as she laughed. "No more, please. I haven't laughed so hard in months." She gasped for air. "Do…do…you show them to a-a-ll your clients?"

Alex shook his head. "You are the first one I've shown them to. Although Abbie probably shared them with Candace and Mandy."

"You're doing it so I feel comfortable talking to you, right?"

Alex nodded. If she continued to be candid with her thoughts, it would make his job a lot easier.

Kimberly bit her lip. "Well, first thing you should know is I don't like bodyguards."

WORDS, ONCE SPOKEN, DON'T RETURN. Kimberly should have remembered the adage before she'd spoken and Mr. Alexander's face had frozen. "Let me explain. All the bodyguards I have known in the past five years have made me feel more like I am a prisoner than protected. At first I thought I could trust them, but I've learned their loyalty is where the money comes from, which wasn't me or my husband."

"Your father-in-law?"

Kimberly nodded. "After Jeremy's 'accident,' the bodyguard thing got worse." She used air quotes. "I'm only explaining because of Candace."

"Accident?"

"Yes, they killed my husband, Jeremy, in a 'single-car drunk-driving accident' on Valentine's Day. I'd texted with him at five thirty. He said he'd be home by six. The accident occurred sometime around nine thirty, fifty miles north, nowhere near our house. He had a lot of faults, but he respected the no-alcohol-in-the-house stance I'd picked up when I lived here with Candace. He rarely drank. He knew I'd made a special dinner. And no one could explain why he was fifty miles north. My father-in-law hinted at a mistress, but I know he didn't have one."

Alex raised a brow.

"I thought he did last year and had him followed. It was all business meetings, my father-in-law present about half the time. Everything was always business. After my third miscarriage, Jeremy was better for a while and the eighty-hour workweeks dwindled to a more reasonable fifty. Then we went on a Thanksgiving cruise, alone." She paused and sipped some water. "He confessed that not all the business practices they were involved in were legal. I urged him to get out. He said he would. Then the eighty-hour workweeks started again. He told me he was meeting with the FBI, the SCC, the IRS, and every other alphabet group. Jeremy wasn't even home enough to realize I had morning sickness. I waited until I was in my second trimester to tell him in case I... He never noticed. I had to hide it from the housekeeper and my bodyguards, but my husband was clueless." Kimberly grabbed the first thing she could off her plate and ate to cover the tears.

Alex quietly waited for her to continue.

"At the mortuary I learned my bodyguard knew Jeremy was dead before the police told me. After the funeral, I realized someone had gone through the house. I had left clear instructions with the housekeeper. My studio was never to be touched, and I put my own clothes away. But someone went through all my drawers and paintings, though they didn't find much. I've become too paranoid over the last year or so, and I regularly check my studio for bugs and cameras. I found one last time they had disturbed things. I told my agent I couldn't work for a while because of Jeremy's death, and I asked him for six months off. He understands."

"What do you paint?"

"I'm an illustrator. I started working under a pen name, or paintbrush name, in college to keep my illustrations separate from my fine art. I kept the name after we married because my father-in-law chided me about my 'little hobby.' Jeremy knew I had some commissions and told me to keep a separate account for tax reasons. I've written a few children's books. I'm glad I followed his advice. My earnings are the only money I have now, and I don't dare access them. I'm down to less than ten grand and a few prepaid credit cards, and I haven't figured how I will pay for a hospital delivery if I'm still in hiding. I am insured through Jeremy's company plan, but my father-in-law would know the second I used my card. Maybe a midwife... Sorry, tangent." Talkative when nervous wasn't a good trait to have when someone who made their living being a good observer sat across the table. He didn't need to know about her worries concerning the baby.

"No problem. So, what does your father-in-law want?"

"I don't know. He asked me where Jeremy put various things, where his safe-deposit box was, what the safe combo was. When I couldn't give him what he wanted, he threatened me. Then he realized I was expecting, and he backed off with the physical threats. However, he doubled my bodyguards. They even started coming into my bedroom. Before Jeremy died, they never walked through the house unless I had company. Now, the only places I could be alone were at the OB-GYN's and the nursery at church. That is no life for me or my baby. I knew I needed to leave for us to be safe. It took me weeks to get everything in place. Then I faked a miscarriage." No point hiding what he'd already heard her tell Candace.

"How is that possible?"

"After having three, I knew how to act. It helped that everyone thought the baby was a New Year's miracle and not a Thanksgiving surprise. A little corn syrup with red food coloring and the bodyguards rushed me and my suitcase to the hospital. HIPAA kept everyone off the maternity floor. The nurse was a friend from church. I asked her to go down the hall and get me some juice, and then I slipped on some scrubs, put my hair up, threw a pair of glasses on, and walked out before they finished my intake information. That was Monday afternoon. Since then, I have been crisscrossing the country using my pen name, maiden name, married name, and two fictitious names. I've spent a small fortune in airfare for flights I missed only to fly on a different flight under a different name. TSA was not impossible to get around. A pregnant woman crying over a stolen wallet works better than it should." Kimberly forced a smile. It would have been comical if she hadn't been running for her life. "I used my real name at airports where I withdrew cash from ATMs. Yesterday morning in Atlanta, I discovered he had frozen my account, so I knew it was time to head here. Jeremy and I initially met in New York. He knew I went to school here but only visited once before we got married. Since Candace had said I was always welcome ..." Kimberly shrugged.

"Do you think Jeremy really was meeting with the FBI or the other groups you mentioned?"

"He said he was, but when I'd ask for details, he'd put me off. I think he knew the walls in our home literally had ears. If I hadn't been pregnant, I think I would have left Jeremy. Our life was too much of a lie. But I wanted our child to grow up with a father." The admission hurt. Kimberly had never said the words out loud, but the thoughts had crossed her mind several times over the past year. "I'm rambling. I guess you didn't need to know my life story."

"Understandable. Have you had anyone to talk to?"

"That I trust? There were a few people I trusted at church, but I didn't want to get them involved or put them in a position where they had to lie. My mother has Alzheimer's. I visited her every other day. Even if I was sure she could have kept the secret safe, I couldn't have told her anything. The bodyguards started lurking around during our visits. I assumed my phone was compromised as we'd tied it to Jeremy's plan, so I took out the sim card and battery before breaking it and tossing it in the garbage on the way out of the hospital. I don't know how my father-in-law got Candace's number and called her from my phone."

"I am sure someone in IT can tell us at least five different ways they could have cloned your phone. How many flights did you take?"

"Enough. I have a collection of peanuts from every airline in the country. I hopped airports too—JFK to La Guardia in New York, DFW to Love Field in Dallas. I didn't have a plan for most of the flights I took. I would just purchase the next ticket I could find to any airport with connections to elsewhere. I changed clothes between every flight, sometimes midflight. At JFK, I cut five inches off my hair, and I have a complete collection of airport souvenir ball caps and shirts."

Alex smiled. "I'm impressed. How did you come up with that idea?"

"I spend too much time watching TV. I love those unrealistic CIA movies and series, and I did the things I'd seen on there. The fake ID was hard to come by. My pen name has credit cards, so she 'lost' her photo ID. I had a duplicate driver's license from when I was single as I lost it more than once. I didn't dare fake a driver's license, but I faked athletic-club memberships, library cards, and employee ID cards to support my missing-ID story. Those pesky graphic-design classes my major required me to take came in handy." Kimberly forced herself to stop talking. "I'm rambling again."

"When is the last time you had a good night's sleep?"

Kimberly thought about it. "Too long ago to remember." Things had fallen apart after the second miscarriage. "Maybe two years ago."

Alex leaned forward. "Two years?"

"That's when things fell apart. Like I said, we didn't have the best relationship. I was his trophy wife, not his companion. I thought if we worked together we could make a better marriage." Kimberly blinked back unexpected tears. "Excuse me." She raced to the bathroom.

Alex started another video call to Candace. It would still be early evening in London.

"Alex? How is Kimberly?"

"Scared. She hasn't told me her father-in-law's name, and I'm still murky on things." Alex inspected the cupboards. The granola bars he found were a year past expiration.

"Hawthorn Thompson."

He recognized the name from advertisements. "Of Thompson Investments?"

"The same. Do you think she is in danger?"

"I think she thinks she is. But it is a definite possibility. How long can she stay here?" He pulled the ice tray out of the freezer. The cubes had shrunken away from the edges and smelled like the fish sticks. Kimberly needed healthy food and rest. And the Art House library wasn't likely to have a book on prenatal care. Abbie might recommend one.

"As long as she needs. I don't know how she is for money. I think her books are selling, but if she is running, it could be a problem. Anything she needs, put on my bill. Can I talk with her?"

"She is in the bathroom. I'll have her call later." As soon as he got her a secure phone.

"We are leaving for a show in ten minutes. I'll text when we get back. If it is an emergency—" Candace looked away from the phone.

"Understood."

"Thanks, Alex." The screen went dark.

Not the usual way he got a new client. But then, not anything about the situation was usual. Beautiful pregnant widows didn't run around doing the cat-burglar-through-skylights thing. Either Kimberly was insane or she was in danger. Or perhaps a bit of both.

Down the hall, a door opened. Kimberly came back into the room. Water clung to the ends of her bangs where she must have splashed her face, and she had applied lip gloss.

"I talked to Mrs. Ogilvie. They were leaving for the theater. She'll call back later."

Kimberly sat back down at the table and attempted to drink from her empty water glass. As she stood, Alex held out his hand and took the glass. Her eyes widened in surprise. Interesting. Even with an absentee husband, she should have had maids and such around her. The default reaction was to expect others to do things for you.

"I'd offer you ice, but the cubes in the trays are pretty old and probably taste like the fish sticks."

"Room temperature is fine."

Alex filled the glass, handed it to her, and sat back down. "Earlier, you told me you don't trust bodyguards because they work for their paycheck. As one of my employers, Mrs. Ogilvie gave instructions for me to keep you safe and to make sure you have what you need. I'll do that as far as you allow me to."

"I don't need a bodyguard."

"Maybe not, but you need a place to be safe. Art House has a state-of-the-art security system."

"Which I broke into."

Alex chuckled. "Which you broke into, thanks to a thunderstorm. The system was also on its lowest level as the house has been unoccupied. Had you changed the thermostat—"

"Not just the doors and windows?"

"Nope."

"Cameras?"

"None inside, and the outside ones are visible. One neighbor stops to wave at them."

"Mrs. Capps? She always used to spy on us. I think I nearly gave her a heart attack the weekend I had dates with seven different guys. She even brought over some of her friendship bread just to ask me about it." Kimberly's smile lightened her face.

"Quite an accomplishment. You also got in here without Mrs.

Capps calling us to report a break-in. She is almost as good as one of Alan's alarm systems." Alex opened his Hastings Security app and made a new pass code for Kimberly. "I am giving you your own pass code for the alarm system. It is unique, so, yes, we can track when you enable or disable it. I'll get you one of the Ogilvie smartphones, and you won't even have to do that. Use your fingerprint. I'll also get you a key. I don't think it's in baby's best interests to continue to use the skylight for anything other than its intended purpose." Alex smiled to reassure her.

Kimberly rubbed her stomach. "I was hoping I wouldn't have to use it again."

"There is a car in the garage. I'll get you keys. So you know, our system monitors the car and, like the house, the car has a panic button linked to our dispatch team."

"The house has panic buttons?"

"Yes. They turn on an audio-surveillance system and patch into our dispatcher."

"Are you listening in all the time?"

"Only if a panic button is pushed or an alarm is set off. You can also set it to record if you think you are in an iffy situation, and someone in dispatch will monitor things."

"So the walls listen too?"

"Only with your permission."

Kimberly nodded. "I can live with surveillance. I still don't want a bodyguard."

Want and need are two very different things. "I can work with that. As long as the threat is low, I'll stay off-site and out of your way."

Kimberly tilted her head and scrunched her eyebrows. "But if the threat is high?"

"My employer is paying me to keep you safe." She'd trusted Candace enough to come here. Would she trust her enough to stay?

"How much say do I get?"

"You can have all you want, and I'll agree unless I think it puts you in danger."

"The phone you mentioned—does it track me too?"

"As in GPS, yes. As in knowing who you called and who you texted, not any more than any other phone." Alex grimaced at his own answer.

"So in an emergency, you can check the last call or text, but my calls aren't monitored?"

"Exactly. How did you know?"

"Too much TV, remember?" The corner of her mouth turned up. "If you aren't with me all the time, how do you know I'm safe?"

"We'll have daily video check-ins. I expect you to tell me your schedule and discuss your outings with me. If I tell you not to go jog in the park, I expect you to listen. If you need to run to the store for milk, I want to know about it before the car shows me it's in the parking lot."

Kimberly leaned back and rubbed her belly. "We accept your terms. Mostly because I trust Candace. You know she would wrap all of her friends in bubble wrap to keep them safe."

"She's gotten better since marrying Colin. Now she only uses a single layer. Next on my list is groceries. Write up a list, and I'll go shopping."

"Bodyguards don't shop."

"Part of keeping you and the little one safe is making sure you are healthy. I've seen the cupboards, and those survival bars are meant only for shipwrecked boaters. You are not desperate enough yet to eat them."

"If I have a car, I can go."

Alex weighed his next words carefully. "You could, but you look exhausted. I'll go."

"I don't have enough cash."

Alex pulled out his business credit card. "It's on Candace."

"But—"

"Sorry, remember, she is my employer. Write me a grocery list, or I'll only buy pickles and ice cream."

Kimberly stuck out her tongue. "No idea how that became a thing. I've wanted ice cream but not pickles."

"Abbie craved orange juice and cracked-wheat cereal for about a week."

"Breakfast foods don't sound so bad."

"No, she wanted them in the same bowl."

Kimberly started laughing. Alex joined her.

"Oh, stop! Laughing hurts."

He clamped his mouth shut and studied her for any signs of distress. "Bad hurt or good hurt?"

Kimberly rubbed her bump. "Not comfortable, not really hurting."

"Still waiting for the grocery list. We need food."

"We? You're not staying here, are you?" Her voice tightened, all traces of laughter disappearing.

"I am staying in town, not at Art House. If you require overnight security, you get to choose a team from the available pool. Given your condition, I'll make sure there is at least one female. We can't protect you if you won't work with us."

Kimberly studied Alex for a long moment. "You are serious? You'll let me choose?"

Alex nodded.

"Then let me write that list." Kimberly dug through a drawer for a pen and paper.

Alex smiled, grateful his new client would not be as difficult as he thought.

THE GROCERY LIST WAS LONGER than it needed to be, but once Kimberly started writing, everything sounded good. The doctor had told her during her last visit that she was underweight and encouraged her to eat. At the bottom of the list, Kimberly added Brownie Sundae and Raspberry Bliss ice cream. She checked the list again, trying to remember if there was some food she was supposed to eat but had forgotten, before sliding it across the table to Mr. Alexander. "I think that is everything."

"Salt and vinegar strawberry yogurt?"

"That should say chips comma strawberry..."

"You intend to eat them together?"

"My version of pickles and ice cream, I guess."

Mr. Alexander smiled. "Mom said she craved straight lime juice with Andrew. I remember seeing her drink it, so I tried it when she wasn't looking. I still don't like lime anything."

"Oh, that sounds good. Will you add limeade to the list?"

He shuddered and wrote "limeade" in neat writing under her ice cream selections. "I won't suggest anything else. It might not fit in the kitchen." Mr. Alexander folded the paper and put it in his pants pocket. "Let me give you a tour of the alarm system, and you can nap while I am gone."

The tour went quickly, as some components were similar to the system she'd used before.

"I expected the panic buttons to be big and red." Kimberly traced the well-camouflaged button in the hallway with her finger.

"Red buttons scream 'Push me.' Not what we want. The idea is to not invite outsiders to notice them."

"I found the one in the loft today. Which I didn't push."

When they concluded the tour, Mr. Alexander held up his phone. "My phone is connected to the app. When I have it on me, I can exit and enter the house without setting or disabling the alarm. I should have a phone for you by tomorrow morning, and you can do the same."

"What about a key?" Not that it would do her much good as he already had one.

"I'll pick one up from the local security contractor while I am out." He patted the pocket that held the grocery list. "Anything else you need?"

Kimberly shook her head.

"Call me if you do." Mr. Alexander left through the front door.

Some security guy. She didn't have his number. Kimberly started back to the bedrooms.

A knock sounded on the door before it opened. "You'll need my number." Mr. Alexander handed her a card. "Make sure you dial the extension too."

When he left, Kimberly stared at the closed door. He'd knocked. Granted, he hadn't waited for her to answer, but he hadn't barged in. If only it were six years ago and he wasn't a bodyguard, she might have convinced him to ask her out. She placed a hand on her abdomen. "Mommy is thinking silly things. It must be those pregnancy hormones. Let's go take a nap."

Her old bedroom had been repainted a cheery yellow. The mattress was one of the new elastic-polymer ones she'd seen advertised on social media. It felt odd to sit on, like dozens of squishy boxes, but when she laid down, they turned into heaven.

The mattress perfectly supported her baby bump without her having to turn at an odd angle. Kimberly barely had time to contemplate the invention before she fell into the first nightmare-free sleep in months.

Alex started his car and punched in the number for Alan's phone.

"Good afternoon, Mr. Alexander."

"Hey, Elle, is Alan still in a meeting? His phone forwarded to you."

"He was just here at the desk. I'll see if I can find him."

"Have him call me back."

The stop at the local security contractor took only minutes. Alex informed them the house was back on active status and Hastings would take over first response as long as a Hastings team was in the area. The company manager frowned as he handed over the only key they had, but Alex couldn't risk them stumbling into the house and finding the feisty woman. Someone would get hurt, and it wouldn't be Kimberly. A vision of her defending herself with the marble rolling pin filled his mind.

If she had been a roommate when Mandy's life was in danger, Alex would have had a hard time focusing. But a pregnant widow on the run from a possibly imaginary threat? It would help if her nose didn't crinkle, but otherwise, the scenario made it easy to be professional. Nothing said unavailable like a pregnant woman. A widow, even. Two Hastings siblings had already fallen for their clients. Alex would not make it a third. Especially not after the hard time he'd given his twin. He got in the car and headed for the old Crawford caretaker's house to see what he needed for groceries.

His phone rang. Alex connected the call through the car's hands-free system.

"ZoElle says you've been trying to reach me." Alan's voice boomed over the speakers.

"There was a break-in at Art House last night. The alarm malfunction was likely because of water in the connection."

"Water?"

"It was raining when the intruder came in through the skylight. Apparently the locking mechanism hasn't worked for years. The installation team must have missed that."

"You are telling me someone entered through the skylight in a thunderstorm? That is crazy! There aren't even any valuables there."

"The wall murals will be worth a small fortune someday if anyone makes the connection between the house and six of the wealthiest couples in the world. Mrs. Ogilvie would never sell." Alex flinched at the thought of someone dismantling the house for the walls.

"Did you catch the intruder, then?"

Alex smiled. "We had a bit of a standoff. She is apparently one of Mrs. Ogilvie's former roommates and attempted to enter using an old key. I gather this wasn't the first time she used the skylight as an entry point. I interrupted the Ogilvie's vacation to ask permission for the intruder to stay." Alex turned onto a dirt road and slowed so the scanner would read his car and open the electronic gate.

"What?"

"We have a new client—Kimberly Thompson, pregnant widow of Jeremy Thompson, son of Hawthorn Thompson of Thompson Investments. You've seen his commercials, right?"

"Wait, you are telling me a pregnant woman climbed in through the skylight in the middle of a thunderstorm?"

"Yup."

"That's—"

"Either desperate or crazy. Maybe a bit of both. She doesn't think her husband's death was accidental and believes her father-in-law is trying to kill her."

32

"I vote for crazy."

"At first I thought she might be delusional as well, except the father-in-law called Mrs. Ogilvie from Kimberly's phone Tuesday. The problem is, Kimberly destroyed that phone on Monday."

"This Kimberly must not have done a good job. And what is up with you not using her formal name? You are the last one to call clients by their first names."

Alex stopped the car in front of a two-story caretaker's house and ran his hand down his face. "It's the best thing to call her. 'Mrs. Thompson' might stress her out more. Anyway, she removed the sim card and the battery and smashed the rest. Makes me think they cloned her phone."

"Sounds reasonable. Anything else I need to know?"

"I need an Ogilvie phone for her, and everything is being charged to Mrs. Ogilvie."

"I think there is a phone in the caretaker's house or in the watch-room at the Crawford cottage."

Alex switched the car feed to his phone. "I'm at the caretaker's now. Let me know what you find on the Thompsons."

"I will. Do you want me to do a background check on her?"

"My guess is that as one of Candace's old roommates, there is already a file on Kimberly. Run a check for the last year. And put a media alert on her. Eventually her father-in-law will do more than call old friends."

Hastings Security kept the caretaker's house stocked with a variety of frozen foods and vegetables. Alex added milk, eggs, and bread to the grocery list. That would do until he decided if he needed a team down here, which would be a problem as few of the Hastings employees were available for an assignment. It would be easier to move Kimberly to Chicago.

And that might not be too easy.

The smell of chicken woke Kimberly. Was it dinnertime? She checked her phone to make sure it was on the correct time zone. Four hours. Kimberly sat up and brushed her hair out of her eyes. She couldn't remember the last time she slept four hours straight. Definitely chicken. She followed the smell to the kitchen. Mr. Alexander wore one of the Christmas aprons Candace's aunt had made for all the roommates one year.

"A bodyguard who cooks?"

Mr. Alexander looked up. "I like to eat, and cooking comes with the territory."

"Oh, I guess it makes sense. Did you make enough for me?"

"I did. My mother taught us it was rude to eat in front of people. During our teen years, she amended that to 'unless it's your brothers in the kitchen.'"

Kimberly laughed. "I can only imagine. I was an only child, so I didn't have any competition for food."

Mr. Alexander checked a small pot. "Dinner should be ready in ten minutes."

Someone had stacked the plates in the cupboard in rainbow order. Who in Art House would have organized the eclectic, hodgepodge dinnerware? Kimberly resisted the urge to rearrange them as she pulled down two plates from different places in the stack. She set her plate at the place where she had illustrated a ladybug picnic and set Mr. Alexander's plate on a flower signed by Araceli. Kim had only met Araceli once, at Candace's wedding. She added glasses of water to the table. There wasn't anything left for her to do. Not wanting to watch Mr. Alexander cook, she checked the fridge. Fully stocked. He'd put away the groceries. No wonder Candace liked her bodyguards.

"Did you want something else?"

Kimberly shut the door. "No, I was trying to remember why I put artichokes on my list."

"Maybe they sounded good?" He turned off the burner. "Do you mind dishing up from the pan?"

"No."

"Abbie teases me saying I get the food decent but fail in presentation."

Kimberly brought both plates from the table and handed Mr. Alexander the blue-speckled one. She hadn't realized she'd chosen one matching his eyes. How embarrassing. Kimberly didn't look at him as she filled her plate, then sat at the table.

Mr. Alexander took the seat across from her. He didn't pick up his fork. Instead he laid his arms on the table palms up. "Do you mind if I pray?"

Kimberly placed her hands in his and bowed her head, mostly to hide her shock. He prayed? And cooked? She pinched herself as the amens were said. Yep. It hurt. So much for still being asleep. The food confirmed it. Kimberly was sure you couldn't eat in dreams and have it taste this good. "Where did you learn to cook?"

"Mom, cooking shows, just around."

"You watch cooking shows?"

"Sometimes." Mr. Alexander used his fork to point at the chicken. "This recipe is one Abbie likes but always ruins. I may have learned to cook it better than her to rub it in."

"Some twin thing?"

"Probably. It may be a sibling—" Mr. Alexander's phone beeped with some alert, his face morphing from relaxed to high alert in seconds. "Your father-in-law is on TV."

Kimberly hurried after Mr. Alexander into the living room. An image of Hawthorn Thompson filled the screen. The banner at the bottom read, "Hunt for Kimberly Thompson!" Kimberly sat on the coffee table and listened to her father-in-law's crocodile-tear-filled voice.

"We don't care what happened. We just want our Kimmy to come home and not harm our unborn grandchild."

At the mention of the detested nickname, Kimberly muttered, "Liar. We? You and who else?"

Hawthorn blinked several times, then cleared his throat. "Kimmy, we understand you are distraught, but we don't believe you killed our Jeremy."

"What?" Kimberly jumped up, wishing she could punch the screen.

The camera pulled back to show Hawthorn putting an arm around a woman he'd been dating.

A commentator's voice took over as pictures of Kimberly filled the screen. "Once again, authorities are searching for Kimberly B. Thompson, widow of Jeremy Thompson, who has recently become the focus of an SCC investigation into Thompson Investments for possible illegal activities, including money laundering and bribery of California officials. We believe Mrs. Thompson walked out of a Northern California hospital after faking a miscarriage. According to her father-in-law, Kimberly Thompson is in the early part of her second trimester. He believes she is a danger to herself and unborn child. She boarded a flight to LAX after leaving the hospital. Authorities assume she is still in California. The family is pleading for the public to help them find her before she can terminate her pregnancy. The FBI wants to question her about her late husband's untimely death. New evidence surfaced yesterday prompting a homicide investigation."

"Unbelievable! I was the one who questioned his death! The police wouldn't listen to me." Where could she run now? The entire country would be looking for her. She could bleach her hair and cut it short. Could she get into Canada?

Mr. Alexander laid his hand on her shoulder. "I believe you."

The three words triggered an internal pause button, her internal tirade subsiding.

He removed his hand and stepped away.

Kimberly circled the coffee table and sat down on the couch.

The news story contained a shot of her pastor, with the church in the background. "We are all praying for her safety. Many of us have been worried about her since her husband's death. She hasn't been herself."

"Only because I wanted to protect you." Kimberly closed her eyes to keep her tears of frustration at bay.

ALEX SWITCHED TO ANOTHER CHANNEL to see the same news conference played from a different angle. They showed a clip of Kimberly at her late husband's funeral. Three men watched her, all of them in military-type stances. Kimberly hadn't exaggerated about the presence of her former bodyguards. They should have been blending in at a funeral, not scaring well-wishers.

When the clip ended, the screen filled with a l-800 number and a text code to report leads.

His phone vibrated. Alan's report filled the screen.

—All major networks, twenty-four-hour news channels, most of the social networks are reporting.

Response?

—Country-wide. How many airports did she get to?

Alex glanced over at the couch. Kimberly clutched a pillow to her chest, eyes closed.

Later

Alex switched off the television and sat down next to Kimberly. "Talk to me."

"What is there to say? I won't have a single friend left. He claims I am a danger to myself and others. And the statement from my pastor. I think they might have edited it. Did you see it jump?"

Alex replayed the few words in his mind. "I think I did. Alan can analyze it and tell us for sure."

"I always thought fake news was about politics and stuff, not about real people. Not about me."

Comforting clients involved in an incident had always been Allie's job. Alex struggled to find the right words. "I doubt any of your friends would believe these lies."

The forlorn expression on Kimberly's face didn't fade.

"How many airports did you pass through before you cut your hair?"

Kimberly used her finger to draw in the air, counting under her breath.

"Nine."

"You changed clothes?"

Kimberly nodded.

"Credit cards?"

"Only prepaid."

"Good. You didn't leave a trail, and you are not showing enough that people would take notice."

Kimberly's hand moved to her abdomen.

"What do you mean?"

Yikes. The one woman rule every man should not ignore. Never offend a pregnant woman. "Occasionally, I've seen an expectant woman in an airport appear so close to delivery I wonder if she should be flying."

Her shoulders relaxed. "I saw two of those. I wondered what the birth certificate would say for location, which state would issue it."

"Probably the real reason they don't want to risk babies born midflight is paperwork. 'Someplace over Kansas' or 'On approach to Denver International'?" His comment earned him a smile. Alex knew his next one would erase it. "We need to make a safety plan."

"I have one. That is why I am here."

"All it will take is one call from Mrs. Capps across the street. Or any private investigator worth the money your father-in-law would spend realizing you lived here and eventually coming to look for you. If you had lived in campus dorms, they might skip the town. But an unoccupied house owned by Candace Ogilvie? Someone will come snooping."

"I don't want to leave." Kimberly rushed out of the room. A door shut with a slight squeak. The far bathroom door's hinge still needed oil.

Alex looked up at the ceiling. He needed more than guardian angels to help with this client. Fortunately, he'd had most of his sister's pregnancy to prepare him for the emotional aspects of this job.

Kimberly leaned over the rim of the bathtub to trace the arm she'd painted years ago. The mermaid bothered her. The proportion of the hand to the face was off by a milli—not enough to matter to most people. It shouldn't matter to her either.

The bathroom had been the wrong place to come to, even if no one in their right mind would follow a pregnant woman into a bathroom. Her stomach was oddly calm, not demanding its usual sacrifice to the porcelain goddess. If she'd been thinking, she would have gone to her bedroom or the loft. Bathrooms needed more comfortable seating. Kimberly lowered herself into the large, empty tub. Fifty gallons of warm water sounded so good right now. But if Mr. Alexander was intent on forcing her to leave, a locked bathroom door wouldn't keep him out. If she had to leave Art House, it wouldn't be dripping wet in a towel.

A little voice inside sounding remarkably like Candace told her Mr. Alexander wouldn't do that to her. Not unless it was a true emergency. He wasn't Jax.

Kimberly inflated an air pillow and put it behind her head. A bath did sound nice. In a jetted tub with a lavender bath bomb. The old seventies blue-metal tub she sat in would have to do.

Funny, the only thing she missed about her house in California was the tub. The studio here was as bright and well organized as her studio there. When she was free to surface, a house with a large tub would be on her shopping list.

What if she was forever ensconced in a prison of protection instead?

Would Mr. Alexander keep her under lock and key? Only if Candace paid him to. Kimberly harbored a suspicion he would try to see to her comfort more than Jax and his crew ever had. That earned him points.

The cheeky pirate standing where the towel bar met the wall caught her eye. When she'd painted him, she'd based him on her then-boyfriend. She'd imagined the pirate as a disavowed duke or the younger brother of a crown prince. But like the model for her pirate, most people were not more than they seemed—they were less.

The inevitable knock sounded on the unlocked door.

"Come in."

The door opened only an inch. "Are you sure?"

"I'm decent." Kimberly didn't bother moving.

The door swung open, and Mr. Alexander tilted his head as he appraised her. "Do you usually sit in empty bathtubs?"

"This is the first time. It is more comfortable than you think."

A corner of his mouth raised in a half smile. "I'll take your word on that. Is it comfortable enough to have a conversation in, or would you prefer another location?"

"The library?"

When every muscle in her midsection suddenly betrayed her and she couldn't find a good hold to get out of the tub, Mr. Alexander extended his hand. "I see the brilliance of your fully-clothed bath method. No awkward help-me-out-of-the-bathtub moments."

"Have you had many of those with clients?"

Handsome as he was, surely some woman had thought of that.

His face reddened a shade. "Not recently. The Ogilvies and

Crawfords are my primary clients. Both women would call their husbands first."

Kimberly grasped his hand. He bent over and placed his other hand behind her back, supporting her as she pulled herself up. As soon as she was safely out of the tub, he dropped his hands, and the feeling of protection left her. The realization caused her to misstep and catch her toe on the rug. Mr. Alexander caught her elbow and steadied her.

Who knew? A bodyguard who actually tried to protect his charge.

ALEX FOLLOWED KIMBERLY INTO THE library. Something about her, maybe the baby, caused him to want to protect her more than his usual clients. Making dinner for her was far from normal. If he wasn't careful, he would fall into what Abbie called his "smothering mode"—something he rarely exhibited with clients. His sister and the few girlfriends he'd had were the only recipients of his smothering.

Kimberly chose a chair. He sat down in the one next to her. "I spoke with my brother. He thinks you should be safe here for a few days as long as you keep out of sight. Who did you interact with getting to town?"

"The shuttle driver. There were eight other passengers, and I got a Lyft from the university. It was pouring, so I had her drop me off at the house after a quick stop at the convenience store, and I paid cash. I used a burner and had a hoodie on."

"Anyone else?"

Kimberly shook her head.

"I don't think Mrs. Capps saw you. She didn't call 911."

Laughter bubbled up from inside Kimberly. "It wouldn't be the first time she's called them on me."

"Eventually she will be by with a loaf of Amish friendship bread and an enquiring mind."

"She still does that?"

"Every time someone is here."

"Then I won't answer the door."

Alex shifted in his seat. "I had planned to stay out at the old caretaker's house at the Crawford mansion, but that doesn't put me close enough if there is an emergency."

Kimberly's lips thinned.

"Normally, I wouldn't suggest this, but would it bother you if I stayed here?"

Her mouth opened, but no sound came out. She shook her head. "You are asking my opinion?"

"Given we are both single and there is no one else in the house…" If he was going to break his own rules of conduct, he needed her permission. Alex ran down the list of employees again. No one could be here by tonight without pulling them from another detail.

"Oh." She squirmed in the seat. "I didn't expect a choice."

No wonder she didn't like bodyguards. "Sometimes you won't have one. But for now, you do. Another option is we both go to the caretaker's house."

"I am fine if we both stay here. The mattresses are amazing." She reddened. "That wasn't an invitation. I mean they're so comfortable—I'm making this worse, aren't I?"

"Don't worry. I know what you mean. The Ogilvies put some prototypes in the house, and they are amazing."

"I have one rule, then. Stay out of my bedroom unless it's life or death."

"Okay. My one rule: stay out of sight, blinds closed at all times."

"Even the studio?"

"Sorry, yes. But you can leave the loft window unshuttered." Not much of a concession, but the chances of even the nosiest of old ladies flying a drone over the house were minimal.

"But I can stay here?"

46

"For now. What is your opinion on Mrs. Capps? Is it better to tell her you are here or let her wonder?"

"I'm not sure. I haven't seen her in years. Candace would know better."

Alex nodded. "I think—"

His phone interrupted them, Candace's ringtone playing. Perfect timing.

"Hello?"

"Hey, Alex. It is after midnight here, but I figured it was only seven thirty there. May I talk to Kimberly?"

"Don't hang up before you talk to me, please."

"What do you need?"

"The situation has escalated, and I wanted your opinion on Mrs. Capps knowing Kimberly is here."

"Mrs. Capps? She snoops with the best of them but keeps a secret like Fort Knox. At least, she kept mine. And she is a midwife, which might be useful."

"Thanks. Here's Kimberly."

Alex left the library to move his truck into the garage.

"Hey, Candace, thanks for calling. Sorry to interrupt your vacation."

"No worries. It is mostly a work thing. Not much different from if we were in Chicago, only Mandy is letting the nanny help so we can go see things without little Joy trying to eat the crown jewels."

"I shouldn't keep you up, then."

"Seriously? Don't make me fly home to hit you upside the head. Now, spill. I saw the news conference. I'm assuming it's all lies."

Kimberly climbed the spiral staircase to the loft. Warm light from the impending sunset filled the room. "Mostly. My father-in-law wants me back, but not because he misses me. I don't know what to do about the whole FBI-wants-to-question-me thing.

I'm not running from the law, just my father-in-law. I'm afraid if I turn myself in—" There was no point in finishing.

"Have you talked to Alex about it? Abbie, his twin in case you didn't know, said something about an uncle with the bureau, or maybe the CIA—I'm not sure." Candace yawned.

"You need to sleep. Don't worry about me. I think I'm in good hands. Your bodyguard is nothing like the ones I had in California. He made me dinner and asks my opinion." Kimberly snuggled into her favorite beanbag.

"Alex cooked for you?" Candace laughed. "I know Hastings Security is the best, but I never heard of one of them cooking for a client."

"So that is weird, then?"

"I'd say. But it goes to prove what I told you. He is a good guy."

"The jury is still out on that. He's a bodyguard. But since you are his client, I guess he can't be too bad."

"He isn't hard to look at either."

"Candace! What would your husband say?"

"He shook his head." A squeak came across the phone line. "And tried to tickle me."

"My cue to go. Night, Candace."

Giggle. "Good night. I'll talk to you later."

"It can wait until you get back. Bye." Kimberly hung up.

The colors of the sunset reflected off a cloud above the skylight. The phone in her hand vibrated, so Kimberly rolled out of the chair and went in search of Mr. Alexander to return it. He wasn't in the kitchen or living room. A noise came from the front corner bedroom.

"Mr. Alexander?"

He came out of the bedroom. He'd changed to a plain T-shirt that was tighter than the polo he'd worn earlier. "Did you need something?"

The word caught in her throat for a second. Candace was right about the eye candy. Those muscles could protect an entire town.

Kimberly held out the phone.

"Thanks." He checked the screen but didn't open it to whatever message he'd received.

"I meant to give you your phone after dinner."

"My phone?"

"It's one of the Ogilvie phones. We use them for our security, and all the C&O clients have them. It is one of many of Mr. Ogilvie's inventions not available to the public. I left yours in the living room." Mr. Alexander raised his arm, indicating for her to precede him down the hallway. He took a slim phone off the bookshelf. "All we need to do is program your biometrics. Full disclosure your phone will respond to my biometrics too."

"Safety precaution?"

"Always." Mr. Alexander guided her through the setup process.

She turned the phone over. "I expected something more complicated than my old smartphone."

"Mr. Ogilvie puts the complicated stuff inside, not for the user to deal with. This is the Hastings app. Your login name is KIMBER. We usually use first initial and last name, but I thought you'd prefer not to use Thompson."

He'd thought of that? "Thank you."

"You can create your own password. Before you agree to the terms of use, understand you are giving Hasting's Security permission to track your location and movements both inside and outside Hastings-secured facilities."

Kimberly skimmed the plain English TOS and checked the proper box.

"Now I need you to choose a word you wouldn't use in normal conversation. If you use the word near your phone, it will trigger an alarm and start recording audio until we resolve the threat."

"Seriously? It's like one of those devices you can ask all the questions."

"Yes, only we won't accidentally order a year's supply of cat toys for you."

Her mind was blank. "I can't think of a word to use. I don't want to use it accidentally."

"I had a client who used *koala* and another who used *pistachios*."

Kimberly ran through words she could remember but wasn't likely to use in conversation. Officer Penguin in her second book came to mind. "Penguin."

"Write it here." Mr. Alexander waited while she typed it in. "Now you need to say your word three times, following the screen directions."

Conversational: "Penguins."

Quickly, voice raised: "Penguins!"

Whisper: "Penguins."

"Now you need to record the word *help*. Most people naturally use that word."

Kimberly recorded the word *help* three times.

"As long as you have the phone with you, it will unlock the doors for you. No more skylight entries."

"I have no intention of climbing on the roof again, at least for the next four months."

"Good idea. Oh, and I put Mrs. Ogilvie's number in your contacts. She will receive your calls now."

"Thanks. Is there anything else?" Kimberly put the phone in her back pocket.

"No. I'm going to the caretaker's house to grab the things I left there. I'll be back in twenty."

"Let me guess. Don't leave the house or open the doors or blinds."

Mr. Alexander grinned. "You're a pro at this already."

Kimberly resisted the urge to roll her eyes until he turned his back.

_____ 🎨 _____

Alex dialed the office as soon as he got in his truck.

Alan answered. "I've been waiting for your call."

"I hope I'm not keeping you from any Thursday-night plans."

"Not in the least." Alan's voice dripped with sarcasm.

"Good." Alex ignored the undertone. "What's the situation?"

"Other than the media conference, not much. The tip line is receiving a fair amount of traffic. No way of knowing whether any of it's credible or what is being reported. The social media posts are all over the country."

"Kimberly hopscotched through a couple dozen airports, changing clothing and airlines. What about FBI involvement?"

"I'm not sure if they are looking for her or if it was the father-in-law making things more dire." Alan's words echoed Alex's thoughts.

"I haven't mentioned going into the Chicago office."

"I'll make a call or two. Uncle Donovan owes us a favor."

"For what?"

"None of your business." Alan's sharp tone set Alex on alert. "What's up?"

"ZoElle's been training with Deidre. Again."

Alex agreed with their sister that the new office manager, whom everyone other than Alan called Elle, would make an excellent bodyguard given more training. "And this is a bad thing?"

Alan grunted.

Alex suppressed a laugh. "Elle will make a good bodyguard. You need to let her grow."

"We weren't talking about ZoElle."

"Fine. About my unexpected client—she's dealing with her lockdown situation better than expected." The electronic gate opened automatically as Alex pulled into the private drive leading to the caretaker's house. "But it would be helpful if we could give Kimberly one or two female bodyguards."

"Deidre is out of the office for a week starting tomorrow." Like many others in the office, Deidre was taking advantage of the Crawford's and Ogilvie's long European trip.

"Is there anyone who's unassigned?"

51

"Not at the moment. And don't even think about asking for ZoElle. She's not ready."

"I agree she isn't ready to lead a team, but she can take a few shifts."

"ZoElle is off-limits." Alan's warning was yet another reason the brothers and Abbie were placing bets on Alan and Elle's potential dating future.

Alex shut off his truck and picked up his phone to continue the conversation. "I'm not desperate enough to go over your head to Dad yet. Kimberly needs a female bodyguard. She is pregnant."

"When is she due?"

"She's at twenty-five weeks. August, maybe?"

"I'll see what I can shift around over the weekend. There's a couple others who have been working with the Ogilvies and Crawfords, but they are taking their two-week vacations to coincide with the month-long trip to Europe."

The call disconnected. Alex only paused a moment before dialing his sister's number. "Hey, Abbie, how ya doing?"

"About as fine as any elephant could be."

"I thought you wanted a gestation period shorter than two years."

"Hasn't Mom told you not to tease a pregnant woman?"

Alex refrained from laughing. "You're the one who mentioned elephants."

"Even walking like a landed whale, I could still take you. What are you doing with your time with the Ogilvies and Crawfords out of the country?"

"I came down to check on an alarm at the Art House."

"Couldn't the locals handle the alarm?"

"I'm glad they didn't. The intruder is an old friend of Mrs. Ogilvie. She entered through the skylight in the loft."

There was a pause on the other end of the line. "I never really imagined the skylight as an access point. It's so small, although Candace mentioned she had one roommate who did it once or twice when she lost her key."

"Add in an Indiana thunderstorm and twenty-five-ish weeks pregnant, and you have one amazing intruder."

"Pregnant? Granted, expecting triplets, I'm larger than your average whale, but even a regular pregnancy—that's hard to envision. She didn't hurt herself, did she?"

"She says no. But I wish she would get a medical checkup. Was there a doctor Mrs. Crawford liked down here?"

"Personality wise, yes. Competency wise, not so much. That's why they came back up to Chicago once Mandy started preterm labor."

Alex put the clothes he had unpacked that afternoon back into his duffel. "That's what I remembered. I don't know that I'll get her into a hospital, anyway. Do you know of any midwives?"

"Mrs. Capps across the street. You know the nosy old lady used to be a midwife. I believe her daughter is one now. They both offered their services when they learned Mandy was pregnant."

"How trustworthy do you think Mrs. Capps is?"

There was a long pause before Abbie answered. "I don't have much experience with her. I know she kept all Candace's secrets. And she makes a mean Amish friendship bread. And she's the type of Amish that drives cars."

"I've been half expecting friendship bread to show up since I came to the house today."

"Unless she already had a batch baking, you're safe until tomorrow morning. I think the starter needs twenty-four hours or at least overnight."

In the kitchen, Alex rebagged the groceries he'd purchased for himself. "I guess I'll ask my new principal how comfortable she is with Mrs. Capps examining her."

"You have a client?"

"Mrs. Ogilvie hired me to take care of our intruder. And told me to spend whatever I needed to."

Abbie's low whistle came through the phone. "Now you have me curious. Who is this acrobatic, pregnant client?"

"Sorry, sis, you know I can't give out a principal's information."

"That's not very nice. If you were in the room with me, I'd throw this pillow at your face."

Alex chuckled. "Hey, you're the one who left the biz. You know that entails some sacrifices."

"Yeah, like giving up my guns—which I will have back as soon as these little cuties are born—and having my twin keep secrets from me."

Given the testy voice, Alex trod carefully. No point in arguing whether she should have her guns back once the triplets were born. Or pointing out how dangerous it could be having guns around three toddlers. After all, he and Abbie had put their mother through her paces, and that was only two of them. "I'll tell you if she gives me permission. You know it's the best I can do."

"Harrumph. I hate sitting here doing nothing all day."

Alex looked around to see if there was anything he'd left. "I'd hardly call incubating my three nephews nothing."

"I owe you a second pillow in the face. I believe that brings me to forty-seven in the last week alone. Maybe I should have a paintball challenge with you once I am up to running instead of waddling."

"Sounds fun. Any tips you can give me for dealing with my new client?"

"Be super nice but don't hover."

"Will do. Night, sis. Love you."

"Is she Kimberly Thompson?"

"How did you come up with her name?" He'd dropped enough clues, hoping Abbie would make the connection.

"Candace invited her to the wedding. Kimberly named the loft."

"You know I can't confirm or deny, correct?"

"You'd deny if you could. I wish you the best of luck with her."

"Anything I should know about her?"

"Only that she named Lover's Loft as a joke, not for actual use. Anything else I know is confidential." Abbie's voice teetered on the edge of a giggle.

Apparently, two could play the client-confidential game. "I'll respect that. I am assuming you know nothing that would help me with her current situation."

"Only that she is more than she seems. Good night, bro."

The line went dead. Alex wished he'd gotten better information. From the moment he met Kimberly Thompson, he'd known she was more than what she seemed.

An unfamiliar chirp awakened Kimberly. She stretched. Her favorite beanbag wasn't the best place to sleep. She checked her phone and found an alert from the Hastings Security app. Apparently it also tracked the employees, as it informed her that Mr. Alexander had arrived at Art House.

Kimberly started down the stairs to meet him. She had questions.

"Kimberly?" His voice came from the front room.

"Coming!" She felt her way across the darkened library. Candace should have listened to her suggestion to put a light switch for the library in the loft. "Oomph!" Kimberly rubbed her shin where it had connected with the coffee table.

The overhead light came on, causing her to blink. Mr. Alexander stood with his fingers on the switch. "You don't need to keep the lights off. Just the blinds closed."

"I know. I fell asleep up in the loft, and there isn't a switch up there." Kimberly sat down on the couch and continued to rub her shin.

He crossed the room and hunched down in front of her. "Are you hurt?"

"Not really. That table and I have a long history. It attacks my shin, I verbally assault it. We repeat the cycle every few days."

He bit his lip and turned his head as he stood. "Your phone has a flashlight mode. Or I could install a motion-sensor light on the staircase."

Of course the phone would have a flashlight, like her old one. "Really? You'd put in a light?"

"Sure, a battery-powered one, but it would be bright enough to cross the room."

"That would be great." Kimberly glanced at her phone. It was past ten. "It's later than I thought."

"My errand took me longer. I stopped by the store to get tooth-paste."

"Oh. Earlier when I was talking with Candace, she said you had an uncle with the FBI. Is that true?"

"Yes."

"I'm not sure what to do. I didn't kill my husband. And I'm worried that if I turn myself in to the FBI, my father-in-law will know." Kimberly rolled the phone end to end in her hands. "I've always considered myself more or less law-abiding, and I think I should talk to the FBI since they are looking for me."

"They are looking for you according to your father-in-law. Alan checked. You are not on the front page of the FBI.gov site or anything."

Kimberly sighed, and her shoulders relaxed. "That's good, right?"

"I think so. My guess is they want to question you."

"Do you think I can talk to them without my father-in-law finding out?"

"Maybe. Would you like to talk with my uncle?"

"Please. I don't like feeling like a fugitive." A yawn interrupted the last word. "I took my second nap for the day. You'd think I wouldn't be tired."

"I think sleeping for two comes with the eating-for-two thing. My sister fell asleep midsentence on the phone with me a few weeks ago. If it hadn't been a video call, I wouldn't have believed it."

Kimberly covered her mouth to hide the convergence of a laugh and a yawn. "I guess I should go to bed, then."

Mr. Alexander stood and offered Kimberly a hand. "Have a good night."

"You too." She took his hand, surprised how such a small gesture made her feel so secure. In just half a day, Alex had completely overturned her opinion of bodyguards.

As Kimberly closed the door, an unfamiliar feeling filled the room. She tried to place it as she changed into her pajama pants and T-shirt. It wasn't until she turned off the light and snuggled into the amazing mattress that she put a name to the feeling. Safe. For the first time in months—no, over a year—she felt safe.

AT THE SOUND OF A door clicking shut, Alex leapt out of bed and into a waiting pair of slip-on tennis shoes, then out the bedroom door, automatically checking for his gun and phone. The app showed Kimberly was still in her bedroom. The living room was clear as he rounded the doorway into the kitchen.

A crash and a scream.

Illuminated by the light of the refrigerator, Kimberly stood with broken glass and splattered milk covering her bare feet, her long hair hiding her face.

"Don't move." Alex turned on the light. "There's glass behind you."

"Sorry. I didn't mean to wake you."

Using the edge of his shoe, Alex nudged a large shard away from Kimberly's feet. "Let me get you out of here." He scooped her up. He could tell from her gasp that she hadn't been prepared to be picked up.

"Put me down. I'm too heavy."

She was actually too light, her ribs too prominent under his hand. He retreated to the living room, where he set her on a chair.

"I could have gotten out of there." Kimberly stood.

"Didn't want to risk you cutting your foot."

"But I could have walked."

Alex stepped out of his right shoe and held it up for her to inspect. A pea-sized piece of glass was stuck in the center. "It wasn't a risk I was willing to take. Check your feet before you go anywhere. There may be a shard on top of them."

Kimberly sat back down and ran her hand over her feet. "Nothing. I'll go put some shoes on and clean this up. You can go back to bed."

She walked out of the room without a backward glance. At least she had the good sense to go the long way rather than through the kitchen. Alex returned to the kitchen and pulled the broom and dustpan out of the pantry.

He was dumping the last of the shards into the garbage when Kimberly reentered the room from the other hallway, shoes on and long brown hair secured on top of her head.

"I said I'd clean it up."

"You did. But I wasn't going to stand around waiting when I could be useful." He set the milk jug and a clean plastic cup on the table.

Kimberly opened the pantry and pulled out a mop, the kind with the disposable pad. "Let me finish."

"Why don't you drink your milk?"

"I don't want milk anymore." She fitted one pad over the end of the mop and lowered it to the floor.

"What do you want?"

"You should rinse out the end of the broom. It got milk in it, and Candace won't be happy if you stink up her house." She pushed the mop up to the end of his foot and veered away.

What did she have to be angry for? Alex poured himself a glass of milk and put the jug away.

"I said I didn't want milk."

"I do." He drained the glass in two gulps, trying to keep from reacting to her waspishness.

Kimberly stopped mopping and pushed a lock of unsecured

hair out of her face. She blew out a breath. "Sorry I snapped at you. I'm just so angry. I broke Candace's freshman glass." She burst into tears. "I'm so, so sorry." The mop clattered to the tile floor as Kimberly covered her face with her hands and spun to leave the room.

Alex reached out to keep her from running into the open pantry door, then pulled her to his chest and let her sob. Abbie had given him some practice in whiplash-inducing mood swings the last couple of months. He rubbed her back and let her cry out her emotions. Every six months, they routinely made videos of all the contents of any protected property. With any luck, there would be a photo and the glass could be replaced.

"I broke her … first one our sophomore year … I never told her … I replaced it with mine. But she" —hiccup—"knew. Hers had a scratch across the school logo and mine didn't. I wanted to keep mine perfect, so I used hers." A fresh stream of tears poured out to be stanched by his damp T-shirt.

"It will be okay." Alex rubbed her back. He'd never comforted one of his clients before. In the rare emergency when it was warranted, his sister and partner had been there for any female emotional support. No wonder his father had cautioned them against being alone with their single clients. Not that his oldest brother had listened. Kimberly was the perfect height, tucked in under his chin. The faster they could assign a female bodyguard, the better. He shouldn't even be alone in the house with this widow, let alone holding her.

Kimberly stepped back. "Now I've ruined your shirt."

"Nah, it will dry. Are you still hungry?"

Kimberly opened the fridge. "Did I put rice pudding on my list?"

No. No pudding. "If you did, I forgot to get it."

"I probably forgot I liked it. Hmmm." She tapped her chin and examined the contents of the fridge, then dove in and grabbed one of the Greek yogurts he'd purchased for himself. "Vanilla. Perfect."

Alex opened the drawer behind him and handed her a spoon.

Kimberly tore off the foil lid. "Thanks for cleaning up after me. I'm sorry I woke you." She tossed the lid in the garbage and exited down the back hallway. "Good night, Mr. Alexander" echoed through the house.

Alex turned off the lights and returned to bed. "Good night," he whispered back into the darkness.

Light beamed through the cracks in the blinds, painting stripes across the covers. Kimberly checked the phone. 9:15 a.m. The last time she'd slept late may have been in this very house on a Sunday during college. She stretched, and her pregnant body demanded she get up immediately. Not fair. No one had pointed out eating for two meant she needed to go to the bathroom for two. Technically, that wasn't exactly true, but it still had to do with the amniotic fluid. Kimberly rushed to the bathroom, hoping Mr. Alexander was in his end of the house.

A spot of blood.

That didn't mean anything, did it? Kimberly pulled up the search engine on her phone. Great. Only hundreds of different answers ranging from "Don't worry," to "Talk to your doctor," to "Rush to the hospital." The last was out. She didn't have enough cash for the hospital, not to mention her not wanting to be identified. According to her research, she needed $5000 for a midwife, leaving about $1000 a month for everything else. If she could get to the rest of her money, there wouldn't be an issue. She should have self-insured last fall. But the medical benefits through Thompson were so much better. Could she add insurance now? She'd wrestled with these questions weeks ago but hadn't talked with her agent or lawyer as they'd need deniability if her father-in-law figured out what she did all day when she "played" in her studio or realized why she and Jeremy had never filed joint tax returns.

Kimberly splashed water on her face. She pulled out an eyeliner pencil and wrote on the mirror.

1. $$—Can I get to any of it?
—Only author account.
—Withdraw $2k a day
—bank will know I am in Indiana.
2. Midwife—Mrs. Capps. Can I trust her?
3. Hospital—Can I go in with no ID?

Should-haves, could-haves, and would-haves filled her mind. None of them helped now. Theoretically, she could use her credit card at the hospital. Like her passport, it was in her maiden name, the one tied to her pen name. She had her business credit card too, but it would give her accountant fits. Midwife first. It would be easier to keep one midwife quiet than an entire hospital, and anything could play on the televisions while she was there.

4. Mr. Alexander.

That problem was a definite wild card. He'd been more understanding and kind than he needed to be yesterday. He was employed by Candace, so his loyalties were nearly the same as hers. But maternity issues were way above and beyond what she would expect him to help with.

Maybe she could ignore the spotting. If it happened again … Kimberly leaned against the counter and hung her head. A new number to deal with. Four miscarriages. To her doctor and husband it was only a number. To her mother it was something else to forget. To her publisher it was three missed deadlines. No one realized it was four pieces of her heart. Waiting wasn't an option. She couldn't part with the fourth or there would be nothing left.

Her stomach rumbled, reminding her it was well past her breakfast time. And time to face Mr. Alexander.

Noises in the back hall tempted Alex to check on Kimberly. He'd expected her up two hours ago. Not that there was any rush. Alan's call this morning brought good news. And after yesterday, they needed some. Alan had grumbled about Elle being approved as part of Kimberly's protection detail, but the rest of the team couldn't be assembled for another two to three days. Jethro Hastings had determined that a small team of three could handle things.

Alex checked his watch. Fifteen minutes. Long enough. He wandered down the back hallway. The bathroom light was on, but the room was empty. Writing on the mirror caught his attention: money, midwife, hospital—and him. He'd never seen a list written on a mirror. Alex turned to leave the bathroom and ran into the writer.

A blush rose up her cheeks. "I was going to erase that." She maneuvered around him and cleaned the mirror with a wipe. "You are probably wondering what you are doing on my list."

"Mildly curious."

"Do you mind if we discuss it over breakfast? I'm starved." She ducked back around him and left the room.

Alex followed her to the kitchen, where she poured a bowl of crisped-rice cereal and milk.

"Do you want anything?"

Alex shook his head and took the seat opposite her.

"I suppose I owe you an explanation."

"Not really. It isn't my business why or what you write on mirrors."

"I think better when I write. Usually I doodle on my lists, but the eyeliner wasn't working for me."

Having witnessed both Mrs. Ogilvie and Mrs. Crawford draw or design when frustrated, Alex wasn't sure he wanted to see Kimberly's version of him.

Kimberly inhaled the bowl of cereal. "It was your yogurt I ate last night, wasn't it? I realized as I finished that I hadn't put Greek yogurt on my list."

"Not a problem. Abbie is always stealing my food. Since she married, I've had too many groceries. Andrew lives with me, but as the youngest, he's learned to stay out of my things."

"You miss your sister, don't you?"

"We lived apart for almost six years when she was in college and I was in the Marines, but we talked every day, other than when I was deployed. Then we were on the same detail as long as we both worked for our dad. It is strange not being her best friend anymore. I get she needs Preston more than me, but sometimes I miss our closeness."

"Do you talk often?"

"Every couple days. When my nephews arrive, it will be less. She will have her hands full." Even with the nanny she'd hired, three children would keep her busy.

"I need to see a midwife."

The sudden change in topic caught him off guard, even if he did have it on his list of suggestions for the day.

She continued. "Mrs. Capps is one. Did you know that?"

"Abbie mentioned it last night."

"I wonder if she could see me today." Kimberly cleared her bowl and filled a water glass.

"Is something wrong?" The shrug of her shoulders while not looking him in the eye indicated there most likely was. "Should I see if she'll come over?"

"We'll have to tell her someone is looking for me and to not say anything. She is Beachy Amish, so she doesn't have a radio or television, just a car and a phone. So she might not know the extent of it." Kimberly played with her water glass, still not looking at him.

"I thought she was one of the older orders of Mennonites since she drove and wore more traditional clothing." No wonder Mrs.

Capps called so often. With no TV, she had nothing better to do than watch the neighborhood.

One side of Kimberly's mouth quirked up in a grin. "I dare you to ask her about the difference."

"Not taking that dare." Mrs. Capps's shorter conversations lasted a half hour.

"Chicken."

"Do you want me to see if she's available?"

"I was going to give her an hour to show up before I sent you over."

"Are you craving her friendship bread?"

"Maybe."

"Anything else you need me to know?" *Why did you have my name on the mirror?*

"Not really. I mean, thank you for being so kind and everything."

"But?" *What is going on? Is it the baby? Should I take you to the hospital?* Sympathy for his brother-in-law filled him. No wonder Preston was a wreck. There was three times as much to worry about.

Kimberly shook her head. "It's nothing. I shouldn't have put your name on the list."

"Would it help if you called me Alex?"

Kimberly tilted her head and blinked.

"I mean, I call you Kimberly instead of Mrs. Thompson. I usually call my clients by their formal names, but in light of things…"

"Candace calls you Alex. What do the rest of your clients call you?"

"Most of them call me Mr. Alexander. Mrs. Ogilvie calls me Alex because she spent too much time with Abbie. I call her Mrs. Ogilvie mostly to annoy her."

Kimberly laughed. "Would you be more comfortable if I called you Alex?"

"You can call me whatever you wish."

"As long it isn't late to dinner?"

66

"More like late when you need a bodyguard."

"Oh." Kimberly turned her back, put her glass in the dishwasher, and started for the back hallway.

"Kimberly?"

She stopped but didn't turn around.

"Are you okay?"

She nodded and kept walking.

Alex frowned. She'd lied. Was the lie a little one or a big one?

SITTING ON THE END OF her bed, Kimberly turned the phone over, wanting to call Candace but not wanting to interrupt whatever amazing thing she was doing in London. A tear splashed on the blank screen. Stupid hormones. Mr. Alexander, er, Alex must think her a complete ninny. Crying because of his kindness again. Not that she'd wish him to be like Jax in a million years. Even before Jeremy's death, Jax had scared her, always watching, always spying. Showing up where and when she least expected it. The tingly horror-movie don't-go-in-there feeling that came with Jax's presence kept her on edge every moment of the day and some nights, when she wondered where he was watching from.

Kimberly laid down and let the tears run their course. For a moment she wished Jeremy was there to hold her. But he hadn't held her in the comforting way she wanted him to since the first miscarriage. Last night, Alex had held her and let her cry. Would he hold her again if she asked him?

The doorbell rang, and something flashed on her phone screen. A doorbell camera. Mrs. Capps stood on the porch with a plate covered in a flour-sack towel. Alex answered the door.

Kimberly checked her reflection in the mirror.

Alex met her halfway down the hall. "Mrs. Capps is here."

"I saw. Do you mind if I talk with her privately?"

"No problem. Let's explain the secrecy around you being here first."

Kimberly nodded.

Mrs. Capps sat on the end of the couch. "Kimberly, right? When did you arrive? I didn't see you."

Kimberly sat in a chair.

"When is the baby due?" The woman eyed Alex suspiciously.

"Not until August. And no, Alex isn't the father. I am recently widowed."

"And you are staying all alone with this handsome man in Candace's house?"

"It isn't what you think. Candace hired him to be my bodyguard."

"Mmm-hmm."

Alex sat at the other end of the couch. He leaned forward, elbows on his knees. "Mrs. Capps, regardless of what you think of the situation, Kimberly is in danger. There are people searching for her using national television, the internet, etc. They may figure out a connection between Kimberly and this house, and it is very important you don't say a word to anyone about seeing her here today."

"Really? So you aren't having a rendezvous?"

Kimberly shook her head. "We met only yesterday. I assure you everything is professional." Well, mostly.

Mrs. Capps turned to Alex. "Then where are the rest of your people?"

"They will be coming."

Mrs. Capps looked from Alex to Kimberly. "And you say Candace knows about this? I'm not sure I believe that. She didn't like your shenanigans with all those guys you dated when you lived here."

"She didn't like me coming home late and waking her up." Or climbing in through the loft window.

70

"Can I talk to Candace? No offense, but I need to make sure you are telling the truth. I won't be part of an affair."

Alex held up his phone. "I'll text her. She is in London. I'll ask her to call if it's convenient. Will you keep Kimberly's being here a secret?"

"Of course I will. I'm not some old gossip." Mrs. Capps raised her chin, adding an inch to her five-foot frame.

Kimberly suppressed a smile. Alex looked intently at his phone and left the room.

"Mrs. Capps, are you still a midwife?"

"I'm mostly retired, but I still help my daughter from time to time."

"I'm worried. I spotted a little this morning."

The expression on Mrs. Capps's face instantly morphed from suspicious to caring. "Anything else?"

"It has been a very difficult few days. Several airplane flights. Climbing in through the skylight."

"Like you used to do when Candace locked you out?"

"You knew?"

"Some of the best entertainment I had was watching the house. But not the best activity for a woman in your condition. Any cramping or pain?"

"No. I've had three miscarriages. I pay attention to anything abnormal." *Please, please don't let this be the fourth.*

"Oh. Let me get my bag. I need my stethoscope. I'll be back in a moment."

Alex reappeared and closed the door behind Mrs. Capps.

"Did you hear?" Kimberly stood and crossed to where she could see his eyes and if he was lying.

He shook his head. "I tried not to."

Kimberly closed her eyes and took a deep breath. "I'm scared something might be wrong."

"What do you need from me?"

"I know it is totally inappropriate, but can I have a hug?"

Alex opened his arms, and she walked into them. Kimberly counted to twenty and stepped back out. "Thank you. Will you show Mrs. Capps to my room when she returns?"

Alex nodded.

"Thank you, Alex. And I am sorry if I made you feel uncomfortable."

He reached out and cupped her elbow. "A hug is never inappropriate when you're scared."

Kimberly nodded, afraid that if she opened her mouth, tears of gratitude would follow. She retreated to her room and waited for Mrs. Capps.

Alex paced the living room and checked his watch again. Thirty-two minutes. How long did these exams take? Finally, he heard the door to the back bedroom open. Mrs. Capps came down the hall, lips pinched. Kimberly followed slowly. Alex wanted to pull her into another hug and solve everything, anything, something, but his gut told him he couldn't solve what ailed Kimberly.

"Kimberly needs an ultrasound today. I'm not qualified to give one. The doctor I usually refer to is not available until next Wednesday. I suggested the hospital, but Kimberly is concerned about being recognized with her insurance card. I have a plan. But you might not like it."

Kimberly sat down on the couch, her face pale. Alex sat next to her and rubbed her back, trying to get her to look at him. She slumped into his side. Something was very wrong. Could this be the same woman who'd held a gun on him yesterday? He turned to the midwife. "What is your plan?"

Mrs. Capps sat down on the chair. "Because of your job, I assume you have excellent health insurance, the kind that covers your spouse the second you get married. If I were to loan Kimberly one of my dresses and a cap, you could present yourselves at the county courthouse and be married in less than an hour. Then you could go to the hospital and register Kimberly as Mrs. Alexander. No one looks too closely at the Amish or Mennonite women, and no one will ask her to remove her cap. Few people can tell the difference, anyway. Even if they notice the earring holes, they won't ask questions and assume she had a wild rum-springa. They'll register her without a social-security number, and your insurance will cover it. I assume you can go online and quickly change it."

Alex didn't want to insult her by asking how she knew stuff about insurance. "Do I have to dress Mennonite or Amish too?"

"No. Your lack of beard can't be easily disregarded, and it is common enough for a woman to marry outside and keep her dress and traditions. The people at the hospital will have seen it before, and those privacy laws will keep them from asking questions."

Kimberly lifted her head. "Are you suggesting we get married?"

"Certainly. It solves all your problems."

"That's not very fair to Alex. He doesn't need a pregnant wife and then a divorce."

"Annulment. I read about it in a book. I'm not sure what the laws are, but you could try that since you are not intimate."

Heat rose on the back of Alex's neck. He pulled a hand over his face, hoping to erase any blush. "What about the baby's birth certificate?"

"Kimberly can still put the father's name on it."

Kimberly stiffened next to him. "I see how this plan keeps me hidden and my father-in-law from finding me, but I can't ask Alex to do this. There must be another way to get an ultrasound."

"I would never recommend them, but maybe in this case ..." Mrs. Capps tapped her chin. "There is a clinic in Elkhart where you can pay cash for an ultrasound. They offer them cheap, as a way to bring people in. Unfortunately, they will try to get you to terminate as they aren't interested in birth options. Rumor says they don't check ID too closely."

Kimberly shuddered. "I can't go there."

Alex knew enough about clinics of that caliber to know he wanted nothing to do with them. He tightened his arm around Kimberly. "Are there any other options?"

Mrs. Capps leaned forward. "Today? No. And I want Kimberly to have an ultrasound yesterday."

"Can Mr. Alexander and I talk about it?" asked Kimberly. When Mrs. Capps didn't move, she added, "Alone?"

"I'll go to my house and find the dress. I sewed it for my daughter. It is a pretty blue. I think you'll like it. The color will match his eyes." Mrs. Capps let herself out.

Kimberly pushed herself away from Alex, then wiped her eyes with a folded tissue.

Alex's thoughts chased around in his mind like the six-year-old soccer team he'd coached last year. Laughing, yelling, and headed for the wrong goal. He took a deep breath. "First, tell me why she thinks you need an ultrasound today."

"Mrs. Capps says I might have placenta previa. Where I have had so many miscarriages, I have a higher chance because of the surgery they use to clean everything up."

"What is placenta prev—?"

"Previa. The placenta is in the wrong place and could detach. This early in the pregnancy, with rest, it can move to a better position as the baby grows. But..." Kimberly didn't finish the sentence.

Alex closed his eyes and prayed. What would his father do in this situation? What should he do? Mrs. Capps was correct. A legal change of name and a disguise would keep Kimberly safe. Alex also suspected that a marriage, even a sham marriage, would give Mrs. Capps some peace that her neighbors weren't "living in sin." He smiled at the absurdity of the thought. He wanted to consult Abbie, though he didn't need to call his sister to know what she would say after she stopped laughing and warned him not to fall in love with his fake wife. "What are the risks of placenta previa?"

"It depends. I am not bleeding much. Extreme cases need hospitalization, sometimes blood transfusions, and the baby is at some risk and may need to be delivered cesarean." Kimberly laid a protective hand on her abdomen, the gesture tugging at his heart.

Thanks to Abbie's pregnancy, he knew having to deliver the baby now would mean a slim chance of survival and weeks and even months of hospitalization. If his insurance could make a difference, there was only one answer.

"I'll do it."

"What?" Kimberly's head shot up.

"I'll marry you, today."

KIMBERLY OPENED AND CLOSED HER mouth, trying to form a coherent sentence. "You can't. I can't. This is so wrong. People aren't supposed to marry for health insurance."

"That isn't the reason I am doing it."

Her hands twisted the tissue in her lap. "Then why?"

"Because it is a brilliant option, and your baby's life may depend on the ultrasound."

He was a nice guy, but next time she married, it would be for the right reasons, not for money as her mother advised. A fake marriage was so risky. "We can go to Elkhart. I won't let them touch me other than getting the ultrasound, and I'll insist on pictures."

Alex shook his head. "No, you are not going to a clinic like that."

Kimberly looked at her phone. "You've known me for twenty-four and a half hours. People don't do this unless they are in crazy romance novels! I can't ask you to do this."

"You didn't ask. I'm volunteering and keeping you safe."

"You can't go around marrying women because you are their bodyguard."

"You're correct. Mr. Crawford and Mr. Ogilvie would be very upset." The smile on Alex's face grew.

"What will your family say?"

"It's about time."

"And when our relationship ends? Because you know it will." He needed to see reason. This wasn't some joke. Just because Mrs. Capps's solution solved several problems didn't mean it was a good one or the only one.

"When it ends, I hope we will still be friends." He gave her a warm smile. If he smiled that way even once a week for the next twelve to fifteen weeks, he'd make it impossible to walk away.

"You can't marry clients because they are widowed and pregnant and need to hide." Kimberly hugged her arms and repeated her argument, hoping to get him to see reason. "This is crazy. We met only yesterday!"

Alex's phone beeped, and he held up a finger. "Hello?"

Kimberly sunk back into the couch and rubbed her head. There had to be another way. Another doctor. Alex was too kind. He'd ruin her for another marriage. In only twenty-four hours he had her believing good guys still existed. Someone out there deserved a guy like him.

Alex tapped her arm and handed her the phone. Candace's face filled the screen. "Alex says you are being difficult. Don't you know the first rule of bodyguards is to never say no?"

"If I hadn't told my old bodyguards no, I'd be a prisoner in the house in California. Sometimes no is necessary."

"Alex would never make it necessary."

"Did he tell you what exactly I am saying no to?"

Candace shrugged. "Not exactly. Just that he had a plan that would help you and the baby and you were being stubborn."

"Stubborn? Mrs. Capps came up with a scheme for me to marry Alex. It is a sham, a marriage of *in*convenience for him, and I'm being stubborn?" Kimberly couldn't help raising her voice. "We've known each other for a day. This will ruin his life. A divorce after only a few months. Any woman worthy of him will think twice and run the other way. It won't matter what his story is."

"He didn't mention marriage. When?"

"Today. So I can go get an ultrasound." Kimberly ignored the knock on the door.

"And this is Mrs. Capps's idea?" Candace leaned her cheek on her hand.

Alex tapped Kimberly's shoulder. "Mrs. Capps wants to talk to Candace."

Kimberly handed over the phone.

"Oh, it's one of those video calls. Don't tell anyone, this isn't approved technology. Did you know your old roommate and your bodyguard were in the house?"

"Yes, Mrs. Capps. I hired him."

"Did you know they were here alone?" Mrs. Capps's mouth formed a thin line.

"I assumed they were."

"Oh."

"And I trust Alex to do his job. Which sometimes requires being alone in a house with a woman. Did you really suggest they get married?"

Mrs. Capps held the phone much too close, poor Candace likely getting an intimate view of her nostrils. "Yes. It is a very sensible course of action."

"I'm sure it is. May I talk with Kimberly again? We are going to go ride the London Eye."

"What is the London Eye?"

"It is a big Ferris wheel. Please hand me back to Kimberly?"

Mrs. Capps handed the phone back.

Kimberly looked around the room. With both Mrs. Capps and Alex there, whatever Candace would say had better not be personal.

"Everyone is listening, right?"

Kimberly nodded.

"You always found an open window when all the doors were locked, and it always worked out."

79

"Even when I broke the lock?"

"It let you in when you needed it the other night, so I consider that working. Okay, I've got to go. Hugs to both of you." Candace smiled a Cheshire-cat grin before the screen went dark.

Mrs. Capps held up a light-blue dress and white cap. "Let's go get you changed. The pins can be tricky the first time."

Kimberly found herself in her room and half disrobed before she could object.

"Do you have any sensible shoes? Those flip-flops will give you away in a second."

"I have a pair of tennis shoes."

Mrs. Capps clucked her tongue. "What size?"

"Seven and a half or eight."

"I'll be right back. I need you to fix your hair like mine. Braid it at the nape and twist it up. Use only six pins." Mrs. Capps placed the last of the straight pins in the dress and hurried down the hall.

"What am I doing?" Kimberly spoke to the mirror.

"Making the right choice?" Alex leaned against the doorjamb. He'd put a sports coat on over his button-down with jeans. "I have a full suit over at the caretaker's house, but it feels a bit too Secret Service."

"I feel like a fraud in this dress. Don't they have some rule against dressing outsiders up in their clothing?"

Alex shrugged. "No idea. I was going to visit Shipshewana one of these days and tour the visitors' center."

The doorbell rang, and Alex left to get it.

Kimberly finished putting up her hair. She hadn't even agreed to this. Why should she? The tiniest of flutters moved inside, and Kimberly pressed her hand to her baby bump. Another flutter. She couldn't feel it from the outside, but someone inside moved. "I hope that means you approve."

"I approve." Mrs. Capps set a pair of shoes on the floor, then fussed over Kimberly's bun and adjusted the cap. "There. Put your shoes on so we can go."

"We?"

"You'll need me as a witness and then at the hospital." A well-worn cross-body bag dangled from Mrs. Capps's arm.

"I feel like I'm breaking some religious rule by wearing your clothes." Kimberly tied the black shoes.

"Didn't Moses hide among the Egyptians and Rahab hide the men of Israel? I am doing the same."

"Won't you get in trouble?"

Mrs. Capps waved her hand in front of her face. "Don't speak unless spoken to, and all will be well."

Alex appeared in the doorway. "What ID do you have?"

"My passport and a birth certificate. My passport is in my maiden name. I got it the year before I got married and never changed it over. Only my California driver's license has my married name. I used my other for business."

"The birth certificate should work. Bring the passport too."

Kimberly unzipped the lining of her suitcase and pulled out the passport. "What would an Amish woman need a passport for? They don't take photos."

"Maybe you converted." Mrs. Capps nodded at both of them. "What are you waiting for?"

Alex offered Kimberly his elbow, and she threaded her arm through it.

"Ready?" He smiled down at her.

"Or not, here I come." She returned a nervous smile, thought of her baby, and let him lead her out the door.

Alex opened the back passenger door of the extended-cab truck for Mrs. Capps and shut it behind her. Then he opened the passenger door for Kimberly. The bouquet he'd picked from the flowerbed around the back of Art House lay on the seat. None of the flowers were roses, daffodils or tulips, but they looked pretty.

A white ribbon he found in the laundry room held them together. He handed them to Kimberly.

"For me?"

"It seemed to me a bride should have flowers, even if…"

"It isn't real?" Kimberly smelled the blooms. "Thank you."

"That first step is too high." Alex scooped her up and set her in the seat, then pulled the seat belt out most of the way. After shutting her door, he tapped the button on his phone to open the garage door.

His phone rang as he turned onto the main road. It was the office. He answered through the truck's hands-free system.

"Mr. Alexander?"

"Hi, Elle. I'm with Kimberly and a midwife in the car."

Elle had worked for Hastings long enough she knew not to disclose any sensitive information. "I checked with the insurance company. The answer is immediately, but you must file a copy of the marriage license in thirty days. Is there anything else, sir?"

"Not at the moment. I hear you will be on my team."

"Yes, unless someone convinces—"

"He won't. I requested you. I think you are ready."

"Thank you, Mr. Alexander."

"No, thank *you*, Elle. And please keep the insurance matter between us."

"Goodbye. You will fill me in, right?"

"As soon as I can. You're on my team, and you'll know everything you need to. Thanks, Elle." The call ended.

"Is she always so formal?" asked Kimberly.

"When she is on the phones at the front desk, she is. We've told her to drop the *sir*, but the more nervous she gets, the more she uses it." Elle would be a perfect addition to the family if Alan would ever do something about it.

"And she will be part of my team?" A hint of nervousness tinged Kimberly's voice.

"Once I have her away from Alan, she'll be fine. He is overprotective, and she tries her best not to have a crush on him. I wager he was near her desk during the call."

"I think I like her already. She sounds nice."

Alex pulled up in front of the 1880s limestone courthouse. As he got out of the truck, he took a quick photo. He helped Mrs. Capps out before opening Kimberly's door.

"I can hop down myself." She scooted to the edge of the seat.

Alex blocked her way. "No hopping until after the ultrasound." He lifted her out of the truck and set her on the sidewalk, then shut the doors and locked the vehicle.

He offered one arm to Kimberly and the other to Mrs. Capps. "Ladies?"

A twinge of guilt followed him into the courthouse. He hadn't even told Abbie that in a half hour, he would be a married man.

The justice of the peace looked bored as she read her lines and waited for the couple ahead of them to respond. This wasn't fair to Alex. Her first wedding had been picture perfect. He deserved the same. Alex rubbed his thumb across her knuckles. She looked up at his smiling face.

He leaned down and whispered. "Don't you dare say no."

Alex led her to the spot in front of the judge. Mrs. Capps stood to the side with a court employee.

Alex turned to face her and took both of her hands in his. The judge repeated the same words she had before. As Kimberly said the appropriate words at the right moment, she worried there might be a special place for women who lied during their wedding wearing the traditional dress of another religious group.

"You may kiss," announced the judge.

"On the cheek." All heads turned toward Mrs. Capp's voice.

Alex bent down and placed a kiss on Kimberly's cheek. "Thank you, Mrs. Hastings." She wasn't sure if the tingle in her spine was from his kiss or her new name.

They signed the papers at the desk in the corner, and a secretary snapped their photo with a Polaroid camera and Alex's phone. Outside the courthouse, Alex asked a passerby to take another couple of photos. He didn't try to kiss her, but he held her protectively close. Kimberly allowed herself to lean into his side and smiled. He would only have one first wedding. She should do her best to make sure the few photos he had were happy memories or at least ones he could laugh at.

He helped Mrs. Capps into the truck first, then came back to lift Kimberly in. She didn't fight him this time. She leaned close to his ear. "Thank you for being the perfect groom. No bride in my position could ask for better." She gave him a kiss on the cheek.

Mrs. Capps directed them to the emergency entrance of the small county hospital and ushered them straight into the maternity ward, where she haled a nurse. "Barbara, Dr. Potts is out of town today, but I would like an emergency ultrasound on Mrs. Hastings right away."

Barbara pulled out a clipboard and handed it to Alex. "Okay, Dad, fill this out while I see about getting your wife a room."

"And some water. I don't think she's had enough this past hour." Mrs. Capps motioned them both into chairs.

Barbara returned with a wheelchair. "Here you go, Mrs. Hastings. Come along, Mr. Hastings. Does Mrs. Capps have your permission to be in the room?"

"Yes." Kimberly sat in the wheelchair.

"Mr. Hastings, make sure you add Mrs. Capps to page three of the HIPAA release." Barbara pushed the wheelchair less than twenty feet into a room, where Kimberly climbed out of it and into a large reclining chair.

"So, what is the problem?"

"I suspect placenta previa. Mrs. Hastings has had three prior miscarriages. With surgery after two of them."

"Dr. Astor is on call. I'll ask him to approve your order." Barbara left the room.

Mrs. Capps handed Kimberly a full water bottle. "Drink until you don't think you can drink any more, then try for another cup. I should have been hydrating you better."

Alex looked up from the papers. "I filled in the easy stuff, like your birthday, which I learned filling out the papers for our wedding, but I don't have a clue about some of these questions." His face pinked.

Kimberly reached for the clipboard. She held in a laugh at the first question. Poor Alex, married an hour and already he had to answer questions about her last period. Kimberly filled in the information and handed the clipboard back.

"Keep drinking." Mrs. Capps shoved the water bottle in her face.

Barbara returned. "Dr. Astor completed the order and says hello to Mrs. Capps. Mr. Hastings, if you'll step out into the hallway, we'll prepare your wife for the ultrasound." She turned to Kimberly. "Would you like him to be present during the procedure?"

Kimberly met Alex's eyes and nodded. He returned the nod. "Yes, please."

"Do you want to know the gender?"

Kimberly bit her lip and shook her head. She didn't want to dream of a little boy who looked like Jeremy. She wasn't ready for that, not while hiding from his father. Mrs. Capps helped drape Kimberly's lower half and pull the borrowed dress up out of the way. Barbara gave Mrs. Capps an odd look. Kimberly realized the nurse must have seen her lacy underwear, definitely not typical Amish or even Beachy Amish, she guessed.

Once only the bump was exposed, Barbara opened the door and invited Alex back in.

Love at first sight was a myth. Unless you were viewing a grainy black-and-white ultrasound image. Every muscle around Alex's heart clenched as the child inside Kimberly stuck its thumb inside its mouth. His hand found Kimberly's. He needed to share the moment. He looked down at her and found her staring at the monitor with the same awe he felt.

Barbara took measurements on the screen. "Baby looks right on schedule for twenty-five weeks. I love the thumb suckers. Have you felt movement yet?"

"Small things, like a butterfly or a hummingbird."

"In another week, Dad might feel something too. Oh, look at that kick. Someone doesn't like me looking into his or her private room." Barbara turned the monitor. "I will do more checking and measurements. Some babies aren't as modest as others, so I turn the monitor to keep the gender secret."

Alex suspected more. Mrs. Capps pointed to several spots on the monitor, and Barbara ran the wand over an area, then another. They held a whispered conversation comprised of frowns and smiles more than words.

"Mrs. Capps, you know the policy. The doctor will review it and give the official diagnosis. He should be here in the next half hour." Barbara switched off the machine, cleaned the gel from Kimberly's belly, and lowered her dress. "Make yourselves comfortable. Mrs. Hastings, there is a bathroom through the door. If you wouldn't mind leaving me a sample in a cup. Mrs. Capps, if you will come with me."

The door closed behind the women, leaving Alex and Kimberly alone for the first time in hours.

"I think Barbara believes Mrs. Capps will say something she shouldn't." Kimberly squeezed Alex's fingers. He'd forgotten they were still holding hands. "Could you give me a hand up? This is an awkward position."

Alex stood and helped her up, steadying her once she was on her feet. "Thanks, Alex."

"No, thank you. That was the most incredible sight. I've seen stills and a video of Abbie's boys. But to see it live—" Alex stopped before his emotions could betray him.

"I am so glad to see her moving."

"You sure it's a girl?"

Kimberly shook her head and walked into the bathroom. Alex tiptoed close to the door, hoping not to hear her crying. When no sobs sounded through the door, he returned to his seat. A knock came at the room's door, and he said, "Come in."

An older gentleman entered. "I'm Dr. Astor. Where's your wife?"

Alex pointed to the bathroom.

"I understand from Mrs. Capps that you were wed earlier this afternoon. Congratulations. I am sorry to inform you that your honeymoon will be anything but traditional. For the safety of your wife and baby, you are not to have marital relations for the next month at least."

Kimberly exited the bathroom, her face pink with color. She'd heard.

"Ah, Mrs. Hastings. I was explaining some restrictions to your husband. You are on bed rest. You may get up to go to the bathroom and sit up to eat. And to take three ten-minute walks a day.

Just around the house, if you aren't spotting. Lie on your left side as much as possible for the next four weeks. At this stage of your pregnancy, there is a good chance that as the baby grows, the placenta will move to a more desirable location. Mrs. Capps knows the drill. In four weeks, come in for a follow-up ultrasound at Dr. Potts's office. Questions?"

"Anything else?" asked Alex.

"No. Just bed rest." The doctor left.

Barbara returned with a wheelchair. "I'll wheel Mrs. Hastings to the front door pickup area if you'll bring the car around."

Alex hurried off, looking for Mrs. Capps as he went.

She sat in a chair in the outer lobby, frowning. "Going home?" Alex nodded.

Mrs. Capps joined him. "Astor kicked me out. Said my credentials weren't up to date. Claims Dr. Potts didn't sign some paper." They reached the truck, and Alex held open Mrs. Capps's door.

She paused before climbing up. "Your mother taught you good manners. I'm glad it is you who will take care of Kimberly."

Alex drove around to the front of the hospital where Barbara waited with Kimberly, then got out and lifted his wife into the front seat. His wife. He liked the word, even if it was only temporary.

HER WILTING WEDDING FLOWERS LAY on her nightstand.

Mrs. Capps finished helping Kimberly out of the dress. "Keep it. You may need to leave the house again." She hung the dress in the closet and set the shoes below it.

Kimberly pulled on her favorite yoga pants and a T-shirt.

"Where are you going?" Mrs. Capps pointed to the bed.

"I was told I could sit up to eat, and I haven't eaten since breakfast."

"Fine, go eat." Mrs. Capps followed her down the hall.

Alex stood in the kitchen, making his lunch. "Do you want a sandwich?"

Mrs. Capps shook her head. "I'll be going now. Take care. I'll check on you tomorrow."

Alex followed her to the front door and locked it behind her. Kimberly eased into a chair, wishing for a nap as badly as food.

"Did you want a sandwich?"

"Right now I'll eat anything without curry or jalapeños in it."

"Turkey, cheese, and tomato on wheat?"

Kimberly bobbed her head and covered a yawn.

Alex set the sandwich in front of her.

"But that's yours."

"I'll make another. You look droopy."

Droopy like her flowers. Kimberly pushed herself up. "My flowers—I forgot to put them in a vase."

Alex set his hand on her shoulder. "Eat. I'll go get them. Where are they?"

Kimberly swallowed the bite she'd greedily taken. "On my nightstand."

He returned a moment later.

"Vase." Kimberly pointed to the cupboard above the refrigerator.

Alex set the flowers in water on the table in front of her. "They look a little sad, don't they?"

Kimberly fought to keep her eyes open. No one had picked flowers for her since third grade when the boy across the street had brought her a fistful of dandelions. "No, they are perfect." The plate in front of her was empty. Had she eaten it all?

Alex cupped her elbow. "Nap time?"

Kimberly nodded and let him lead her down the hallway. He pulled back the comforter and tucked her in, then punched several keys on her phone. "I've set this so it will alert me if you say anything."

Without opening her eyes, she tried to reply, "Thanks."

There was the soft brush of his hand across her brow before exhaustion took over.

Alex cleaned up his lunch and stared at his phone. Mom, Dad, or Abbie? After a moment, he dialed Abbie, not wanting a video call.

"Hey, what's up? Two calls in two days. Need more pregnancy advice?"

"Not exactly. Who is with you?"

"Mom."

Alex rubbed the back of his neck. "Better put me on speak-erphone."

"Done."

"Hi, Mom."

"Jethro said you found a new client," said Mom.

"That is one way of putting it."

"Alex, what is wrong?" Abbie's voice held a note of panic.

"Nothing is wrong. I kind of got married today?" He couldn't keep the questioning tone out of his voice.

"What?" He couldn't distinguish his sister's voice from his mom's.

Alex held the phone away from his head and their scream.

"How do you kind of get married?" asked Mom.

Alex explained the events of the day, including the Beachy Amish dress and the ultrasound results.

"Do you remember all the lectures you gave me about Preston last year? I was only pretending to be his fiancée. You married your principal." Abbie hung up and immediately called back on video call.

Alex's thumb hovered over the answer button for a moment. Not taking the call would be a mistake. "Yes?"

Both his mother's and sister's faces appeared on the screen. "Son, marriage isn't a thing to play with."

"I know, Mom. But it felt like the right thing to do. Kimberly kept telling me not to, and she had good reasons, but it felt right." How lame was that? But it was the truth.

Mom grew quiet. "You're sure about this?"

"Yes." There was no question in his mind. For better or worse or only fifteen weeks, this was the right thing.

"Are you planning on a divorce?"

"Or an annulment."

Mom shook her head, and her face left the screen.

"Where did Mom go?"

"She went in the other room."

"How upset is she?"

"Do you have to ask? I think you topped the list of stupid things done by her children. But she is torn. On the one hand, you say it felt right, and they've always told you to follow your gut. On the other hand, Mom and Dad have worked hard to show us what marriage can be like, and you get married in some sham."

"I know, but, Abbie, you've got to believe me. I'd do it again if everything were the same."

"I do, Alex, I do. But I am not sure how I feel about this. You didn't even tell *me* until after. I need to go."

The screen went dark.

Alex leaned back and stared at the ceiling. For the first time, he doubted his choice.

"Idiot!" A man's voice roused Kimberly.

"Calm down. So help me ..." a female voice responded.

"Both of you quiet down before you wake her." Alex's voice was only a decibel or so quieter than the other two.

"I haven't seen Mom so upset—"

"Hush!" said the woman.

Kimberly rubbed her eyes. Not another bad dream and not the television. Curiosity pulled her down the hallway and to the front room.

"Alan, Mrs. Hastings said no fighting." The woman sounded desperate.

Crash!

Kimberly hurried the last few feet. A man lay on his back on the floor, the coffee table on its side. A woman not much taller than Kimberly stood with her hands on her hips. Alex stood near the door, unsuccessfully holding back a laugh. His eyes met hers, and he bounded across the room to her side.

The man on the floor sat up and glared at the woman. "Who taught you that?"

Alex slipped a supportive arm around Kimberly, staying between her and the others in the room. Kimberly leaned forward to see the commotion.

"Your sister and Deidre and every one of your brothers." She didn't change her stance. "I warned you."

"But I didn't think—"

"Precisely. Like you didn't think before you started yelling at your brother or threw a punch."

"But you're supposed to be on my side!" The man stood up. One of the Hastings brothers. His hair was darker and his skin paler, but there was no mistaking the resemblance.

"No, I am supposed to be on the detail to protect Kimberly, who is clearly standing here when she should be on bed rest!" The woman turned and extended a hand. "Hi, I'm ZoElle, or Elle for short. Everyone but Alan and my mom call me Elle. Sorry about the noise. Shall I send these two outside so we can have a chat?"

"Is that safe?" Kimberly directed her question to Alex.

Alex looked at his brother. "I don't think that will be necessary. Everyone can act like the adults we are supposed to be. Kimberly, this is my older brother Alan. Apparently, he felt the need to rush down here and check on things. Elle had the good sense not to let him drive alone." Alex turned to Kimberly. "Do you need anything?"

Kimberly held up her finger and slipped out from under his arm. She would not announce her need to go to the bathroom. When she returned, the coffee table was back in place. Alex pointed to the recliner. "I brought it up from the basement so you had an extra place to rest."

Under the scrutiny of the bodyguards, Kimberly sat down and immediately reclined.

Elle sat on the end of the couch nearest Kimberly. "We were discussing dinner. Alex wasn't planning on company, so Alan is buying. We were debating between pizza and burgers. Alex says the Chinese place around here can be iffy. What would you like?"

"My vote is for pizza." Kimberly smiled at Elle. Whatever history she had with the brothers, it was obvious she could handle them.

Elle cast a satisfied look at the men. "What is your favorite topping?"

"Spicy food and I aren't getting along, so Canadian bacon and pineapple?"

Alex and Alan made faces.

Kimberly tilted her head to look Alex in the eye. "Is that a problem?"

"Not as long as we don't have to share."

"Then it's settled. Alan and I will go get the pizza." Elle dragged Alan out the front door.

Alex crouched down beside the recliner. "Sorry about the yelling. Alan is usually our mild-mannered computer nerd, but when something hits too close to his heart, he loses it."

"He is upset you married me?"

"A little. I think he is more upset he's attracted to Elle and won't admit it. He's been a pain for the last five months."

Kimberly scrunched her eyebrows together. "So he likes Elle and is mad at you?"

"Elle was his client. Alan doesn't leave the office much, but one fateful day he answered an emergency call, and they've been dancing around each other for months now." Alex laughed. "The look on his face when she threw him."

"So I read the situation right. How did she do that? She is so small compared to him, and she put him flat on his back."

"I'll have her demonstrate. It's one of my sister's signature moves. Elle perfected it a few weeks ago. I was the first on the receiving end, but it was on a mat in the gym."

At the fluttering of her baby, Kimberly moved her hand to see if she could feel the movement outside.

Alex covered her hand with his. "Is something wrong?"

"No, I can feel the baby moving on the inside but not with my hand yet. I'm sorry I am causing you grief with your family."

Kimberly turned to look at him.

"Not really. Abbie is mostly annoyed because she can't meet you. Her doctor has her on modified bed rest. She called an hour ago and tried to get me to bring you up for a month-long pregnancy slumber party. My parents understand my choice too."

"Understand doesn't mean agree."

"It doesn't mean they disagree either. It just isn't what Mom envisioned."

"I can't imagine any mom planning for her son to marry a pregnant woman dressed in Amish garb. Maybe had a nightmare about it ..." The annulment couldn't come too soon.

Alex laughed. "It sounds funny when you put it that way."

"You know those lame get-to-know-you games?"

"Like two truths and a lie?"

Kimberly nodded. "After today, you will always win."

Alex brushed a hair out of Kimberly's face. "I have a lot of good ones from today. A nurse kept calling me Dad, and I got to hold your hand and see this little one." He patted the hand Kimberly covered her baby with, then looked away. When his gaze returned to hers, Kimberly was sure there was an extra layer of moisture in his eyes. "When this is all over, may I be an honorary uncle?"

"I would like that very much. After all, you loaned me—I mean, us—your name to protect us. You may have full uncle rights and privileges." An if-only ran through her head, but she pushed it away.

"So I can spoil the kiddo rotten and buy too much junk food at Cubs games?"

"Definitely." Kimberly licked her lips.

Alex's eyes followed the movement. "Well, I am not being a good uncle now. I'll be right back with a water bottle."

Kimberly watched him leave. He deserved to be so much more than an uncle. She prayed the right woman would see past the quick marriage and divorce. So many women ran at the mention of the D-word assuming it meant damaged goods.

THE NEXT MORNING, ALAN GRUMBLED a goodbye but didn't resist Alex's bear hug. "Are you more upset about my marriage or about leaving Elle here?"

"ZoElle will be fine. There haven't even been any credible tips at the Indianapolis airport on social media, and I suspect you won't have any problems here for a few days. If they'd figured out the link between Kimberly and the Art House, they wouldn't still be looking in California. They are still working on the airplane trail." Alan sounded like he was trying to convince himself.

"You're sure?" Alex didn't like waiting for some unknown thug to show up.

"As sure as I can be. I'm not the FBI or law enforcement, so I have less to go on."

"Speaking of which, Kimberly is willing to talk to Uncle Donovan officially. I need a plan to get them together." As tired as Kimberly had been last night, he wasn't ready to make her endure the three-hour drive to Chicago.

Alan opened the front door of his SUV. "I'll let him know. Watch out for ZoElle."

"Elle is ready for this. I know you still see the woman you met last year, but she had uncommon strength even then. She faced down the world only a few days later. Trust her."

Alan shrugged. "I know she does well in the gym, but—"

The door between the garage and the kitchen opened, and Elle stuck her head out. "Kimberly's father-in-law is on the morning show. You'd better get in here."

Alex sprinted across the garage. "Does she know?"

"She's watching it in her room."

Alex jogged down the hallway. Maybe putting a TV in there last night wasn't such a good idea. Kimberly sat in the middle of the bed, blankets piled around her. She wiped away a tear with the corner of the sheet. Alex sat down next to her and pulled her into his arms as the face of her father-in-law filled the screen.

"That is a good question, Dave. After following several tips, we believe our dear Kimberly may be suffering from a delusion that she is Leigh Benz, the popular children's book author, or she is merely impersonating the author."

Kimberly gasped and grabbed Alex's shoulder.

The morning-show host commented. "Could she be Leigh Benz? We've tried for the last two years to get her to come on when we've done our holiday show as her books are always featured, but her publisher always declines. To the best of my knowledge, no one knows who Leigh Benz is."

Mr. Thompson laughed. "My daughter-in-law just doodles. I've seen her studio. She thinks she is an artist, but she couldn't sell a landscape in one of those traveling art shows."

Kimberly stiffened. "I knew you were spying."

The female host looked mildly uncomfortable.

"Don't get me wrong." Mr. Thompson smiled into the camera. "I love her little doodles, as did my son. He loved her, which is why we are so desperate to find her and the grandchild she is carrying." He held up a photo of Kimberly, and the camera zoomed in.

"We'd like to remind our viewers of the tip line. Kimberly Thompson, widow of Jeremy Thompson of Thompson Investments, is missing." Several photos, including a wedding shot, rotated across the screen. "Law enforcement does not suspect foul play. However, her family is very concerned, especially now that Kimberly's mother, Marsha Benoit, was admitted to a San Francisco hospital in critical health after a fall and we've yet to hear anything from Kimberly." A 1-800 number and a text code filled the screen. "Now, for a word from our sponsors."

Alex took the remote from Kimberly and clicked the mute button. "What else did they say?"

"My mom fell. I don't know how that was possible. She hasn't been out of bed for weeks. I think they did something to her to make me come out of hiding. I knew this was a possibility, but I didn't think he'd do something so soon." Kimberly leaned into him.

Alex adjusted his position so he could hold her and let her recline.

"Don't worry, I will not be stupid and call her. Mom hasn't recognized me for the last several visits, so there isn't much point. She has insurance through her retirement, and I set up a fund to supplement it. I can only pray she passes quickly if that is what is happening. I knew when I went into hiding that she might die in the next few months. I've said my goodbyes."

Alex debated acknowledging the tears he saw in her eyes. The way she blinked and turned her head he guessed he would embarrass her.

"What else?" Alex asked Alan, who was typing faster than should be humanly possible into a tablet.

"The same as last time mostly. I'm mentally unstable. FBI wants to talk to me. They found my pen name. I used Leigh's credit card for a few of the tickets. I probably should contact my lawyer and my agent." Kimberly reached for her phone, but Alex covered it with his hand.

"That can wait." He looked to Alan and Elle standing in the doorway. Alan still tapped away at his tablet. Elle's mouth hung open.

"You are really Leigh Benz?"

"Yes. That's why I didn't change everything to my married name and I've filed my taxes separately. Jeremy knew I made 'a little,'" Kimberly made a one-handed air quote, "from my illustrations, and he told me not to invest it with the firm or commingle our accounts. About three years ago, he asked me not to tell him anything about my "side business," as he called it. He always played it down to his father as my hobby."

Alex looked to Elle for guidance.

"Not that I am prying, but aren't you making a few million a year?" asked Elle.

Alex tried not to react. He'd suspected she had some money and even a secret, but he hadn't calculated over a half million.

"Only ten last year, but it's hard to get to now. It would require going into a branch bank and showing ID, which my father-in-law has made impossible. Before my escape, my bodyguards watched my every move. I didn't self-insure because Jeremy had such good insurance. So that is how I ended up here, with only $10,000 to my name. I haven't used my business credit cards so my accountant doesn't have to lie."

"When you told Candace you'd pay her back, you were serious." Alex wanted to be sure he understood.

"I was, and she knew it. But my measly millions mean little to her." Kimberly smiled and rolled her eyes.

Alan looked up from his computer. "Did you take a shuttle bus from the Indy airport?"

"Yes."

"I think we need a new plan. I have no idea how long it will be before they get to the tip someone just posted on the social media page saying you got off at the college."

Kimberly was shaking now, and Alex pulled her tighter to his chest. He looked at his brother. "Give us a minute?"

Kimberly rested her hand against Alex's heart. It wasn't racing as fast as hers was. "Sorry about the surprise. I was going to tell you about my job before I told the FBI."

Alex moved again and settled Kimberly into the bed, then slid off and knelt by the side so they were face-to-face. "Anything else I should know?"

"I'm hungry?" She touched his shoulder. "I'm sorry. I was going to explain better last night, but then your brother showed up, and your parents called, and I came in here and hid. Even though it was technically our wedding night, I didn't think Alan would approve of you coming in here for a talk."

"He's probably annoyed I am in here now." Alex tucked the blanket around Kimberly's shoulders. "But that isn't your problem. Do you think you can survive a ride to Chicago? The front seat reclines some, and I can put a box under your feet."

"Could I lie down in the back seat?"

"You could, though it isn't the safest way to ride, and I'm afraid it will be more uncomfortable."

She would rather sit next to him than behind him. It would make it easier to talk. "Where would you take me?"

"There are a couple of options. My sister's offer for a sleepover works. There is a small guesthouse on the property if you want privacy, and she has a nurse-midwife come in to monitor things every few days. I'm sure we could ask her to check on you too. Her security is run by another firm as good as ours. The advantage is the isolation."

"She isn't going to deliver the triplets at home, is she?"

"In her dreams. But until then, she hates IVs, and having the nurse come check on her prevents her from turning the doctor's office into a three-ring circus should someone recognize her from one of the tabloids."

"Makes sense. How will her husband feel about me staying in the cottage? Won't I endanger her?"

"Between us and Simon Dermot Security, that's not very likely. And your father-in-law will have to make a few more connections before they even look at Abbie and Preston's place." Alex swiped at his phone and smiled at what he saw. He turned the phone to face Kimberly. One of the wedding photos from yesterday filled the screen. "The you in this photo barely resembles the one being splashed across the media."

Kimberly pushed the phone away. "I look terrible."

Alex shook his head. "Maybe a little pale and worried, but the no-makeup look works for you. But that isn't the point. No one seeing you dressed like this yesterday would link you to yourself. It will take days for the county recorder to get the marriage certificate entered into the public record. Unless they are looking, they won't notice whatever announcement gets stuck in the local newspaper. Abbie's place is much safer than here."

"But I don't want to bring my problems to her." The fact that she'd married Alex was bad enough. Putting his sister in danger was unforgivable.

"If Abbie and Preston agree, will you go?"

"Only if you make me breakfast." As far as she could tell, she didn't have a choice, so food was a bonus.

"Done."

Kimberly reached for her phone as soon as Alex left. It wasn't there. She sat up and looked under the pillows. He must have taken it. Kimberly changed clothes and threw her few belongings into her suitcase. Someone tapped on her door. Kimberly opened it to find Elle on the other side. "I have strict instructions to only let you get dressed and use the restroom. Alex is worried about you doing too much with the drive today."

"I've been reading online, and I think the doctor telling me to stay on full bed rest was a bit extreme."

Elle held up her hands. "I am a bodyguard, not a doctor. Perhaps you can get a second opinion in Chicago. Mrs. Crawford raves about her doctor, the same one Abbie uses. Now that you have access to Mr. Alexander's insurance, it shouldn't be a problem."

Kimberly sat on her bed. "How upset is the family, other than Alan?"

Elle folded a T-shirt. "Mr. and Mrs. Hastings are contemplative about it. Mr. Adam, he is the oldest and is on tour with his fiancée. He didn't seem to care too much other than ribbing Mr. Alexander for getting married first. Abbie really does want to meet you. I'd put her as curious. To be honest, Mr. Alexander isn't impulsive, and an elopement, even for a marriage of convenience, isn't his style. Mr. Andrew is in Europe. I don't know how he reacted. But he'll support Mr. Alexander."

"What about you?"

"I'm not part of the family."

"But you have an opinion."

Elle bent down to pick a pair of socks up off the floor. "I think he did the right thing. Mr. Alexander is a nice guy, and—"

Alex appeared in the doorway with a tray. "Eggs, toast, and juice. Abbie and Preston agreed. I spotted Mrs. Capps out the window. I don't know what she will think."

As if on cue, there was a knock on the front door. Alex set the tray on the desk and jogged down the hall.

Mrs. Capps bustled into the room. "I see no problem with going to Chicago. In my opinion, the doctor overreacted. I would have told you to avoid bending, lifting, running, and marital relations, although I assume that last one isn't an issue in this marriage."

"Then why didn't you contradict him?"

"Child, you are all wrung out. And dead on your feet. I wanted you to rest for a few days. I was going to tell you tomorrow. If there isn't any bright-red blood, don't panic. If there is, get yourself to a doctor or hospital, preferably not our county, as soon as you can.

Placenta previa almost always clears up on its own." Mrs. Capps turned to go and patted Alex on the arm. "You keep helping her in and out of your big truck, though."

Alex followed the midwife down the hall.

Kimberly stood and pulled her sweatshirts out of the closet. When this was over, she'd have to do something nice for him. She had at least fifteen weeks to figure out what.

ALEX CARRIED KIMBERLY'S THINGS INTO the guesthouse. Elle would come later. Preston had requested that Hastings furnish at least one bodyguard at all times. He and Elle would trade shifts for now. Elle would take days, and he would have nights.

Kimberly came out of the bathroom, where she had practically run from the truck. "Wow, this place is amazing. I pictured something smaller when you said cottage. This is almost as big as Art House."

"There are two suites on this floor. Abbie says the yellow one has a mattress like the one you like at Art House. She fell in love with hers months ago and is putting them in every property she has."

Kimberly hid a yawn. "I don't know how it is possible to be tired still or again. All I did on the drive over was sit and talk."

Stress? Alex hated to add to it, but her phone conversation with her literary agent and lawyer were not as simple as he hoped. That Uncle Donovan had agreed to meet that afternoon wouldn't help. Alex wondered how long he could wait to broach the subject. His phone rang. "Hello, Abbie."

"I saw you arrive. Can you come over for lunch?"

"Can we make it dinner? Uncle Donovan wants to speak with Kimberly."

Kimberly came out of the bedroom and tilted her head, clearly listening.

"Okay. Dinner, then. Bye." Abbie disconnected the call.

"Who wants to talk to me?"

"My uncle—the one with the FBI. The sooner they can state that they have spoken with you, the sooner they can end the media mess your father-in-law is causing."

"When?"

"As soon as you feel up to going to his office. They'll patch a secure conference call through to the investigator in California."

Kimberly dusted off her T-shirt. "I wish I had something more appropriate to wear."

"Abbie jokes that she grew out of half her maternity clothes between the words *two* and *three* when the doctor told her about the triplets. She might have something you can borrow."

"Are you in the habit of loaning out your sister's clothes?"

"Twin." Alex tapped in Abbie's number. "Hey, can we come over now? Kimberly wants something other than an oversized airport T-shirt to wear to the FBI."

Alex held out the phone so Kimberly could hear. "Oh, I have scads of clothes. Come and take your pick."

"We'll be right up."

Kimberly shook her head. "Do you always do that?"

"What?"

"Solve nonexistent problems. I really didn't need to borrow her clothes."

"But you said—" Alex paused at Kimberly's frown. "I guess I do. I can call her back and cancel."

"After the excitement in her voice, never. But consider this our first marital argument. Don't do everything for me."

That was a fight? "Sorry. Do you need anything before we go?"

"I need a bit of makeup. Will you put those bags on the bed, please?"

Alex put her bags away and retreated to the main room. He

didn't have to wait long. He'd never seen Kimberly in makeup. She was pretty before, but the addition of whatever had made her eyes more stunning.

"You're staring. Is something wrong?"

"No, nothing. Right now you would definitely be recognized as the photo on TV."

"I'll take that as a compliment. Amazing what hiding the dark circles under my eyes can do."

Alex offered his arm and escorted Kimberly to the house.

The FBI office was what she expected and less. Kimberly removed her sunglasses and the floppy hat matching the pink floral maternity dress Abbie had loaned her. Abbie insisted pink was the best choice as it was feminine and vulnerable. Alex's twin knew enough about color theories to be dangerous. Kimberly had chosen the dress for another reason—one Alex would not like and might try to forbid if he knew.

After they pinned on their visitor badges, a young man in a generic blue suit showed them to an office marked "Deputy Director Hastings." A gray-haired man stood as they entered, and shook Alex's hand, then Kimberly's. "Water? Coffee?"

"Just water, please." Kimberly sat in a chair designed to look comfortable while it kept its user on edge.

"In a few minutes, we will go into a conference room where Kimberly will talk with the agents from San Francisco. Alex, even though I understand you are now her husband, you get to stay here." He turned his focus back to Kimberly. "From what I understand, the questions are a follow-up to the questions you raised after your husband's death. You are not a person of interest in his death. We will record the conversation as it is being cast via closed circuit. Do you have any questions?"

Why didn't you believe me before I disappeared? "Not yet."

The younger man in the blue suit appeared at the door and nodded.

Kimberly followed him down the hall. The conference-room chair was more comfortable than expected. On the screen in front of her, a younger man and woman sat in a room like hers.

"Agents, this is Kimberly Benoit Thompson and, as of yesterday, Hastings. Which makes her my nephew's wife, so yes, there is a relation, but since this case is not mine, I have no conflict of interest. I will sit in." Deputy Director Hastings's voice was one few could ignore and hopefully not dispute.

Agent Danes responded first. "Yes, Deputy Director. Hello, Mrs. um..."

"It may be simpler to call me Kimberly."

"Thanks, Kimberly." Agent Garcia tucked a hair that had fallen out of her bun behind her ear. "Our first question is, why did you contact the FBI after your husband's death?"

"Because I thought you might know more than I did."

"Why is that?"

"Jeremy told me he was meeting with agents because not everything at work was honest."

"When did he tell you that?"

Kimberly disclosed what little she knew, the twenty-questions thing getting old fast. "Last Thanksgiving, Jeremy and I took a cruise—no other family, no bodyguards. We needed to be alone. I was trying to decide if I should file for divorce. Our marriage had gone downhill since we moved to California three years ago. I couldn't decide if it was work or my father-in-law. During our discussion, Jeremy told me that not everything was legal and promised me he would go to the ... SCC, I think? I told him I would stand by him if he was trying to do the honest thing. A few days before Christmas, we went to look at lights at this park, and Jeremy quietly shared with me that he'd met with the FBI too. But he wouldn't give me any details because he didn't want his father knowing and the bodyguards were watching. He told me it was safer for me not to know, and we couldn't talk about it in the house. After that, he hardly spoke to me. He worked late and had odd arguments with his father. Jeremy was so distracted he didn't even realize I had morning sickness. On Valentine's Day, I called him at the office and told him I'd prepared a special dinner. I was going to tell him about the baby. He said he'd be home in a half hour. As you know, he never made it. He didn't drink around me and only rarely for social events. He knew I didn't like him drunk. He would not have driven to Oregon drunk, and not when he'd promised to be home in half an hour."

Alex's uncle handed her a box of tissues.

"You are sure about the time you called him on February 14?"

"Very sure. I didn't want the chicken to be dry. I had an ultra-sound picture to show him. We'd lost three babies before. I'd never made it to twelve weeks. I looked at the clock a million times as I waited. The bodyguards knew he was dead before the police told me. They shouldn't have known."

"You're sure they knew?" asked Agent Garcia.

"Jax told me I needed to answer the door and talk to the police, then stayed and waited while I talked to them. I thought nothing of it at the time, but it was as if he knew I would faint as I do far too easily during the first weeks of my pregnancy. My bodyguard confirmed it at the funeral home. Gave me one of the superior looks he always did when he knew things. Of course, the staff and bodyguards knew what my husband didn't because they watched me all the time."

The two agents exchanged a look.

"I know it sounds paranoid, but they did. After the funeral, it got worse. My father-in-law kept asking if Jeremy had left a key, or a letter, or something. Then, one day, I found a camera hidden in my studio. Someone had been through my paintbrushes. I am very particular about them. And yes, I am Leigh Benz. My attorney and agent can verify that for you."

The passive look on Agent Dane's face slipped for a moment.

"Then I realized someone had also gone through the drawers in my room. The bodyguards even started staying inside the church with me. It had been the one place I could be me."

"One day, I came home and discovered that the books in the library had been rearranged, and I found another camera. It took me three weeks to work out an escape. If you all didn't want to talk to me, I would still be out there." Kimberly pointed in the direction of the door.

"You are sure your husband never gave you a contact name or anything?"

"He didn't. I don't think we spoke more than a few sentences after Christmas, and it was always the same thing. Either 'I'll be late' or 'Sorry, I'm late.' He even stopped sleeping in our room because he 'didn't want to disturb' me."

"Director Hastings said you got married yesterday. Wasn't that fast?" asked Agent Garcia.

Faster than you'll ever know. "Are you asking if I was ever unfaithful to Jeremy? No. I didn't meet Alex until recently. And yes, it was a very short engagement." *Less than two hours.*

"Well, if your husband married you for your money, he might not see it anytime soon."

"Why?"

"We are taking steps to freeze all of Thompson's holdings, including any accounts in your name."

"The money I get writing and illustrating as Leigh Benz was never commingled with my husband's. He had no idea how much money I have. We filed separately. I didn't even use his investment firm. Is it to be frozen too?"

The two agents looked at each other. "Sorry, ma'am. Your funds will be frozen as well. You understand we keep finding new accounts and they need to be examined."

"Why? It should be obvious from Hawthorn Thompson's interview this morning that he has no clue I am Leigh or how much money I've made in the past five years."

"Just for the duration of the investigation."

"I earn thousands of dollars in royalties a day. Will I be able to access those funds when my check arrives at the end of the month? Part of my reason for talking to you is so I can come out of hiding and access my money. In case you haven't noticed, I have a growing responsibility."

The agents looked at each other. Alex's Uncle spoke. "As I understand it, Leigh Benz is under contract with one of the big New York publishers. Are any of them under investigation?"

"No, sir."

"Tell me, in your investigation, has Leigh Benz's name ever come up?"

"No."

"Then I suggest a forensic accountant go over the Leigh Benz accounts in the next few days. If all the funds in the accounts match those from the publisher and have been reported properly to the IRS and not commingled, as Mrs. Hastings has told you, her funds can be unfrozen as soon as possible." Deputy Assistant Director Hastings carried an air of authority. Kimberly wanted to stand at attention and shout 'Yes, sir!'—and he wasn't even addressing her.

"We will need to talk to our assistant deputy director about that," answered Agent Danes.

"I am sure you will. I expect that with the cooperation of Mrs. Hastings and her lawyer, clearing her funds shouldn't take long at all. Do you have any more questions for Mrs. Hastings?"

The agents shook their heads.

Kimberly leaned forward. "I have one. For days, my father-in-law has been appearing all over the media insinuating everything from me being insane to the FBI wanting me in connection with my husband's death. I would like your help in clearing my name. When I am done here, I intend to walk into one of Chicago's affiliate TV stations and have my own little news conference. I would like someone to make a statement that I am not a person of interest. I don't need every doctor I see thinking they are dealing with a felon."

Agents Danes and Garcia nodded.

"We can do better than that. We can call the press conference from our press room downstairs if you would like," said Alex's uncle.

"That would be much better. I am eager to clear my name."

Agent Garcia leaned forward. "You will still need to be careful. We don't know who killed your husband or his FBI contact."

The room went black.

Alex studied the books on his uncle's bookshelf. Not the collection he expected. Intermingled with subjects ranging from forensic DNA studies to famous FBI cases was a full set of C. S. Lewis books, including the Space Trilogy. The same agent who'd shown him into the room interrupted his snooping. "Deputy Assistant Director Hastings would like you in the conference room. Follow me."

Kimberly sat in a chair with a blood-pressure cuff on one arm and a half-empty single-serve bottle of orange juice in her other hand.

"What happened?" Alex asked.

Kimberly opened her mouth to answer, but Uncle Donovan beat her to it. "The agents in California wanted to gauge your wife's reaction to certain information. They failed to consider her condition, and she fainted."

An agent removed the blood-pressure cuff. "Probably dehydration and low blood sugar. But I would call your doctor." She handed Alex a sticky note. "Her pulse and blood pressure from when I first arrived and now. Your wife's OB might want it."

Alex crouched down in the spot the agent had vacated at Kimberly's side. "How are you feeling?"

"Stupid? Embarrassed? I knew I should have eaten more at your sister's, but I was worried it wouldn't stay down. When they"—Kimberly looked at Uncle Donovan—"said certain things, I learned something I've always wondered about: it's possible to faint while sitting." She attempted a smile and rubbed the center of her forehead.

Alex brushed her fingers aside and checked for any signs of swelling. "Do you need ice?"

"No, I'm good."

"Let's go back to my office," said Uncle Donovan.

Alex helped Kimberly stand, then put his arm around her waist. "I can walk."

"I know, but I'm going to play the concerned husband and keep my arm around you." The comment earned him the faintest elbow in the ribs, but she didn't pull away.

Uncle Donovan closed the door to his office. "Have a seat." He opened a mini fridge. "I have a turkey sandwich, some string cheese, a tuna—no, it's from Monday—an apple, and strawberry yogurt. If nothing sounds good, I'll order something up."

"The turkey sandwich, please."

Uncle Donovan handed her the sandwich and a water bottle before sitting down behind his desk. "Do you want to go ahead with the press conference?"

Alex appraised Kimberly. "What press conference?"

Kimberly ignored his question and spoke to his uncle. "Yes. The sooner I can call off the search for me, the sooner they can use those resources to find people who are really missing."

"Do you know what you want to say?" Uncle Donavan leaned on his desk.

Kimberly held up her phone. "It's on here. May I turn it on?"

His uncle nodded. She turned on the phone, opened an app, and handed it to Uncle Donavan, who scrolled through the page. "Well thought out. You may need to change one thing with the freeze on your assets, though."

"I think I can leave the line. It says "Leigh Benz had committed to donate." It doesn't say when the donation will occur. I have full confidence the account can be cleared quickly."

The frown on Uncle Donavan's face showed he didn't agree, but he didn't argue. Questions formed themselves into a list in Alex's mind.

His uncle handed back the phone with his card. "Email that to this address. I can get it printed off, and you can turn your phone off again. I'll arrange for the press conference at the top of the hour." He turned his laptop around and tapped on his keyboard.

Kimberly shut off her phone. "That's in only twenty minutes. Is that enough time to get the reporters here?"

Alex wanted more details. Why hadn't Kimberly consulted him? Obviously, she'd done more than text during the three-hour ride to Chicago.

"More than enough time." Uncle Donovan pulled a paper off his printer and handed it to Kimberly, simultaneously picking up his phone. "The San Francisco office was supposed to send over a press statement. Agents Danes and Garcia, can you let them know we need it ASAP and we go live at 1500 our time, not theirs? Tell them I'll make something up if they don't send it. Thank you."

Kimberly dropped her sandwich to her lap. "Can you do that?"

Uncle Donovan waved his hand. "Press releases are mostly boilerplate. I can quote what yours will say within a couple words. Basically, it will say thank you for your cooperation and list pertinent details about your husband's death and ask for leads. It will also affirm you are not a person of interest, regardless of your father-in-law's insinuations."

Someone tapped on the door.

"Enter."

The young agent from earlier handed Uncle Donovan a paper.

"San Francisco field office sent this over."

"Thanks. Ten minutes till showtime. There is a bathroom through that door. I'll be back right before we go down." Uncle Donovan left.

Kimberly stood, and Alex caught her hand. "Was the press conference their idea or yours?"

"Mine. I planned it on our drive up here. The sooner I can come out of hiding, the better for everyone. I know I may still be in danger from whoever killed Jeremy, but this way, no resources will be wasted trying to find and protect me. And you won't have to pretend to be my husband anymore." She closed the bathroom door before he could say anything.

Alex stared at the door. She better not think she could be rid of him with a press conference. Not until her husband's killer could be found and her father-in-law dealt with. As for the annulment, too much had changed in the last twenty-four hours for him to want one. He froze at the thought. He needed time with Kimberly to be sure.

Once Deputy Assistant Director Hastings finished the official FBI statement, Kimberly took a deep breath and stood behind the podium. Thankfully, it was solid and big enough to hide her shaking knees. Alex stood against the wall behind her with two agents, including the one who had administered first aid earlier.

"Over the past several days, there have been television interviews and news conferences with my father-in-law, Hawthorn Thompson, claiming many things, from questioning my sanity to my involvement in my late husband's death. I would like to address his claims. I did not disappear or go missing.

"I ran.

"Every person has the right to run from an abusive relationship to find safety. I felt it was in my best interests, as well as that of my unborn child, to seek shelter outside my father-in-law's sphere of influence. I am in a safe place. Please stop searching for me. There are those in this country who are truly lost. Please put your efforts and resources toward finding them. Because I left, my father-in-law has called my mental health into question, claiming I am delusional or deeply troubled and unfit to be the mother of my child.

"It is not delusional to want to be safe. Seeking safety for myself and my unborn child proves I am a fit mother. Deputy Assistant Director Hastings has already addressed my cooperation with the FBI and the suspicious death of my husband. I will remain in contact with him and his associates in law enforcement throughout the investigation.

"Another claim has to do with Leigh Benz. Yes, that is my pen name. A separate press release is being made this afternoon by my agent regarding a donation to several organizations that provide shelter to the abused and reach out to find the lost. In some small way, I hope to shift the focus of media and the resources that have been unnecessarily spent on me to those who desperately need such help.

"I thank everyone who turned in tips for their concern. Please put your efforts toward helping others around you. Thank you." Kimberly stepped back from the microphone.

The reporters shouted over each other.

"Mrs. Thompson, where have you been hiding?"

Kimberly took another step back and found Alex's hand, clinging to it as the questions continued.

"Will you return to California?"

"Does the FBI have any leads on your husband's death?"

Deputy Assistant Director Hastings stepped between her and the microphone. "We will not be taking questions. There will be a copy of this press release on the FBI website within the hour. Thank you and good day."

Alex led Kimberly out of the briefing room, flanked by the two agents.

Alex's uncle showed them into a small waiting room and shut the door. "The two of you can wait here until someone shows you out. Most of the reporters will run to file their stories before the East Coast news airs."

Kimberly extended her hand. "Thank you for all your help."

"A word of caution: Agents Danes and Garcia think you know more about your husband's activities than you've admitted to, most likely something you don't realize you know. They will want to question you again, in person."

"I'm not going to—"

Deputy Assistant Director Hastings held up a finger. "If they believe it, then whoever killed your husband probably thinks the same. I suggest you keep yourself in whatever safe house Alex chooses. I didn't disclose your change in marital status to the media to help with that." He turned to Alex and held out his hand. "I need to return the suit coat."

Alex shrugged out of the suit coat that had been tossed to him moments before they entered the briefing room, then handed it to his uncle and was enveloped in a hug.

"Congratulations on your nuptials. I feel I should remind you that insurance fraud is a crime the bureau takes seriously. I trust your marriage will last a very long time. I'd hate to investigate my favorite nephew. Oh, and Agent Samuels thinks your wife should see a doctor soon if she hasn't already had a glucose test for gestational diabetes."

Kimberly swallowed her gasp as Alex's Uncle left, and then she sank into the closest chair.

Alex laid a hand on her shoulder. "Are you feeling light-headed?"

"Yes, I mean no. Insurance fraud? I never—"

Alex bent to eye level. "It didn't even cross my mind."

"What have I done?"

The following week, Alex held Kimberly's hand in the doctor's waiting room as she gulped the last of the orange, syrupy drink. He tried not to laugh at the face she made.

"I'm sure they would let you try some. It's like the orange drink the fast-food places sold when I was little, only concentrated."

"No, thanks." Alex scanned the waiting room again. No one was paying attention to them. They'd settled into a routine over the past week. During the day, Alex went to work as normal, only he kept to office assignments. Elle or another bodyguard spent the day with Kimberly at the cottage or over at the big house with Abbie. At night, Alex returned "home." No one in the Hastings family ever referred to the temporary nature of the marriage. Kimberly hadn't mentioned it, but when she fell asleep in front of the computer, he noticed she had been researching annulments and insurance fraud.

The FBI had yet to release Leigh Benz's accounts, but Alex found he wasn't in any hurry for Kimberly to gain financial independence. Instead, he wanted to be celebrating their one-week anniversary. After all, they'd survived Mother's Day at his parents' house with all the crazy looks, which had been as difficult as standing behind her during the press conference instead of at her side.

He probably would not have thought about their anniversary had Abbie not texted him. One-week anniversaries were a thing? Didn't most newlyweds take at least a weeklong honeymoon? When he searched the internet, he found only ideas for the one-year anniversary: paper or clocks.

"Mrs. Hastings?" A nurse clad in pink scrubs called from the doorway.

Kimberly held on to his hand as she stood, giving him a little tug. He raised an eyebrow, asking if she was sure. Kimberly gave him the slightest nod. Alex followed her back to a bench where the nurse checked Kimberly's blood pressure and temperature before sending her into a small restroom.

"So, Dad, how are you doing? You look a little uncertain. Is this your first appointment together?"

Alex checked his stance and realized he was in full-alert bodyguard mode. He willed himself to relax. "No, I was there last week when she had an ultrasound."

"Did you find out the gender or decide to keep it a secret?" The nurse marked something on her tablet.

"We want it to be a surprise," answered Alex.

Kimberly emerged from the restroom, and the nurse showed them to an exam room.

The nurse checked her tablet. "I see we received your ultrasound results from last week. Since they diagnosed you with placenta previa, the doctor will not do a full exam today." She looked at Kimberly. "As long as she can get where she can listen to baby's heartbeat, you can keep those clothes on."

The tension seeped out of Alex's shoulders. The room was too small for him to give Kimberly privacy if she needed to change. Thus far they had avoided seeing each other without clothing, other than the baby bump during the ultrasound.

"Dr. Song should be in, in a minute." The nurse closed the door as she left.

"You don't need to look so relieved." Kimberly climbed up on the examining table.

"I don't want to invade your privacy." Alex perused the basket of magazines on parenting and Hollywood gossip. One of the magazines had Kimberly's picture on the front. Out of curiosity, he picked it up. The magazine had definitely doctored the image. He held it up for Kimberly to see. "I think the photographer believes you're having six or seven children. They must have used the same filter they did when Preston and Abbie announced they were expecting triplets. Those photos were scary."

Kimberly covered a laugh with her hand. "Yesterday afternoon, Abbie and I had a lot of fun surfing for photos of her. Abbie thinks it's hilarious so many people are interested in her pregnancy. That photo isn't even bad. There's one we dubbed 'elephant mama.' Neither of us think it's humanly possible to get that large."

"Good thing. I wouldn't be able to refrain from making jokes."

"Abbie loves it when you tease her. You shouldn't worry so much about offending her. Or me. If you don't crack at least one or two jokes when I waddle, I will wonder if you are fit to be the baby's uncle."

There was a tap on the door, and the nurse came in with a box full of equipment to draw blood. "Your twenty minutes is up. It's time to take the second blood draw."

Like last time, Alex stood at Kimberly's side and held her hand. Kimberly kept her eyes on him the entire time. She barely winced as the needle went into the vein.

"All done." The nurse gathered the tube of blood and put another bandage on the inside of Kimberly's elbow, then left.

Alex remained holding Kimberly's hand.

"Thank you. That's the worst part of these visits. It's also one reason I want to have a home birth."

Alex nodded. His knowledge of the different birthing options was almost as big as his knowledge of brain surgery or rocket science. "Another thing you have in common with Abbie. Although she doesn't get much choice."

Someone tapped on the door again. An Asian woman with a stethoscope around her neck entered, the embroidery above the left pocket of her lab coat announcing she was Dr. Song. "Kimberly Hastings?" She asked Kimberly for her date of birth before sitting down on a rolling stool. She looked up at Alex. "I watch enough evening news to guess you are not the father of this child. Am I correct?"

"Yes."

"Will you step out of the room for a moment?"

Alex met Kimberly's eyes, and she nodded. Alex exited the room, the door shutting behind him. He stared at a painting of a mother and child on the opposite wall. Out of habit, he counted how long the door had been shut.

After what seemed like forever, the door opened and Dr. Song beckoned him to come back into the exam room. "Kimberly is adamant you be allowed in on her appointments."

Kimberly reached out her hand, and Alex circled the table to take it. The doctor sat down and looked at the computer. "You are considering a home birth?"

"That is my plan. I understand my placenta previa could change that."

"If you went into labor now, at twenty-six weeks, it would definitely change things. But in another ten to fourteen weeks, statistically, the placenta should move, and you wouldn't have a problem. I have two nurse midwives on staff. Would you like to meet with them?"

"No." Kimberly bit her lip. "I have someone in mind. I have spoken with her. But if I can't do a home birth, I'd like you to be in charge of my delivery."

"I can work with that. We'll schedule another ultrasound in four weeks—give this little one time to grow and see if the placenta moves." Dr. Song took a boxlike device not much bigger than her palm out of the drawer. "Let's see how baby's heart is doing." Dr. Song set the handheld device on Kimberly's stomach and moved it around. Within seconds, the room was filled with the whop-whop-whop of a human heart. Dr. song smiled. "Your little one has a good, strong heart."

Alex tried to swallow. He had never heard a sound like that. He looked down at Kimberly and found her smiling. Dr. Song pulled a measuring tape out of her pocket and measured Kimberly's baby bump. "Perfect. You can sit up now."

Alex placed his free hand between Kimberly's shoulder blades and helped her up.

Dr. Song typed into her tablet. "Someone will call you about your glucose test tomorrow. Do you have any questions for me?"

"Just one." Kimberly scooted herself closer to the end of the table. "Last Friday, when I had my ultrasound, the doctor said I needed to be on bed rest for several weeks. Is that true?"

"Have you had any bleeding since last week?"

"No."

"You don't need to be on bed rest. However, I would suggest not lifting anything heavier than a gallon of milk. Leave the laundry to someone else; get someone to pick up anything you drop." Dr. Song moved her focus to Alex during her last statement. "No marital relations."

Alex felt heat rising at the back of his neck. Kimberly blushed.

"I would suggest you go on several short walks a day, nothing strenuous. Avoid hills. And not a mile each. And make sure you're eating regularly. I tell most of my patients it's fine to eat like a hobbit: eat first breakfast, second breakfast, eleven o'clock snack, lunch, and so forth. Several small meals with both a protein and a carb is preferable to three big ones. You are slightly underweight, I assume from how sick you were during your first trimester. An ice cream cone or three a week is on your suggested list for sugar and calcium, providing your glucose test comes back normal. Any questions from you?" Dr. Song addressed the last question to Alex.

Alex had dozens of questions, but it was highly unlikely Dr. Song knew any of the answers.

Kimberly set her paintbrush down. She'd painted more over the last three weeks than she had all year. Between the Harmon's normal security, Elle, and Alex, she felt safer than she had in forever. So she was sleeping, and the characters flowed from her paintbrush. She turned the painting over. Dr. Stork was perfect. She debated about naming the doctor after an old wives' tale. Mama bunny wore maternity clothes to balance the narrative. The working title, "Bunny Gets a Brother," needed tweaking. She'd let the editor have a go at that. This was the fifth time she'd started this book. And the first time she felt confident in finishing it.

Elle stuck her head into the screened porch area where Kimberly sat. "I'm off. Alex is at the front gate. See you tomorrow."

"Have a good evening, Elle." Kimberly waved without fully turning around. Elle wasn't getting much practice being a real bodyguard unless bodyguards sat around all the time. A few minutes later, she heard Alex cross the kitchen and come out onto the porch. Dipping her brush in the vermillion, Kimberly didn't bother hiding what she'd been working on as she had with Jeremy.

"Dr. Stork, I presume?" At the rumble of Alex's deep voice, warmth spread through her soul.

"Do you think it's too cliché?" Kimberly picked up her thinnest brush and dipped it in indigo.

"I can't say I've read a lot of children's books in the last thirty years. Other than the ones I've read of Leigh Benz this week. I wouldn't worry. Your characters thrive on the cliché."

"You've been reading my books?"

"I wanted to see what the mystery side of your life looks like. Abbie had ten of them in the library. I think she is missing one."

"No, you read them all." Jeremy had only read the first book, the one she'd published six months after they got married. Since most children's book authors, in fact, most authors, failed to live above the poverty level on their author income alone, Jeremy had cautioned her against being too optimistic and told her to keep the money she made in her own account so she could buy a few things now and then. Three weeks later, she'd had her first miscarriage, and Jeremy had never asked about the books again. "My life isn't mysterious. I write out a rhyming story and doodle on the page."

"You do more than that. You weave difficult scenarios into your books. I'm assuming Candy the Otter is based on Mrs. Ogilvie."

"Candace wanted a story about cancer and terminal illness she could read when she visited the children's hospital. She wasn't thrilled I named my otter Candy."

"I think it's my favorite so far. A bald otter wearing a feathered coat."

"I liked the knitted turtleneck shell." A picture of a big, protective bear named Alex formed in her mind.

"Abbie is hosting the family dinner at her house this Sunday. Dr. Song has told her not to go very far. We're invited."

"I know. She called and invited me earlier. I still feel like a trespasser. Your family was so kind to me on Mother's Day. I know you've been avoiding it, but we need to talk about what we will do later." Kimberly stood and went to clean her brushes. "And I've been doing a lot of research. I think if I come clean and pay the insurance company, you shouldn't have any repercussions—if the FBI ever gives me back my money."

"That reminds me. Uncle Donovan called to let me know the FBI received another email from your father-in-law. It's addressed to you."

"I don't want to see it. Let them do whatever they want with it. I called Mom's hospital today. She's still in ICU. They can't find her living will, so I asked my attorney to fax a new copy." Kimberly kept her back to Alex, knowing if she turned around, it would take only one step to find herself engulfed in the bear hug he always offered and the tears would come.

Alex stepped closer. She could feel his heat on her back. He laid a hand on her shoulder. "If you want to make it happen, we can get you out there before she passes."

Kimberly shook her head, biting back the sobs that would start if she opened her mouth.

Alex reached around her and removed the brushes from her hand, then turned her to face him. "You'll have both Hastings and the FBI watching your back."

Kimberly closed her eyes. More than missing her mother's death and funeral, the kindness in Alex's face tore her apart. She shook her head and sidestepped him. He let her pass.

Other than to insist she eat, Alex left her alone the rest of the evening. While she ate, he walked the grounds. Not that there had been a single threat in the three weeks at the property. It hadn't taken her long to realize how Alex used his job as an excuse to give her space when he thought she needed to be alone.

Kimberly washed the dishes by hand, hoping Alex would return. He didn't.

She climbed into bed and texted him. **Good night. Going to bed early.**

—Sleep well.

She should stay up and make him talk about their marriage before it got more confusing. Alex saw more about her than she expected. He bought her favorite ice cream, listened to her babble without laughing, and let her fall asleep on his shoulder. The truth was, Jeremy never paid this much attention to her unless it was a corporate event and she had parsley between her teeth. She'd followed Mom's advice and married for money, believing it would last. Next time, she'd marry for love. Money wasn't worth it. If only she could marry Alex next time.

Beep. Alex sat up at the first note of the alarm from his phone.

"Alex?"

Beep, beep.

Kimberly never used the audio feature in the night.

"What's wrong?"

Alex rolled off the couch and slipped on his shoes.

"The"—hiccup—"hospital"—hiccup—

Alex opened Kimberly's bedroom door without knocking.

"She's gone." Kimberly sat in the middle of the bed, wearing one of last year's Hastings softball team shirts.

In two steps, he crossed the room and pulled her into his arms.

She cried.

And cried.

When Kimberly fell asleep with her head on his chest, Alex tried to slide her off, but she grabbed a fistful of T-shirt and mumbled something sounding remarkably like "Don't leave me."

So Alex stretched out beside her, and Kimberly burrowed into his side. He wrapped an arm around her and counted the clicks of the ceiling fan. He'd leave as soon as she fell into a relaxed sleep. He wouldn't notice the scent of lavender or the tiny sighs.

He wouldn't text Uncle Donovan to ask that they slow up the forensic accounting so this could last longer.

Early morning light peeked above the window ledge. A pressure on her side pushed her out of a happy dream. She fought to get the dream back, trying to remember what made her so happy. The pressure lessened, and her brain urged her to wake up to understand the messages it was receiving. Automatically, her hand went to explore, expecting to find a twisted comforter, but instead, she found a hand.

The hand moved, sliding out of her grasp.

Kimberly rolled onto her back.

"Sorry, I was trying to leave without waking you."

Alex? Memories of last night returned. The phone call from her mother's doctor. Alex holding her as she cried. Kimberly asking him to stay.

She reached for him and caught his hand. Something—there had to be something she could say to make the moment less awkward. He didn't move, the faint light of dawn casting most of his face in shadow. How could she explain how badly she'd needed his comfort last night or how amazing it felt to be cared for?

Kimberly opened her mouth, willing her tongue to move. Instead, something, or rather someone else, did. "Oh." She brought her free hand to her abdomen in time to feel another kick strong enough to be felt from the outside.

She removed her hand and guided Alex's to the same place.

His eyes widened, as did his smile. "Does this happen often?"

Kimberly laid her hand over his to keep him from moving it. "This is the first time the kick has been strong enough to be felt outside."

"You've felt something before?"

"Fluttering, like a butterfly with a case of hiccups."

The baby pushed against Alex's hand, and he lifted it. "I don't think he likes me restricting his space."

"I think I'm the one restricting *her* space." Kimberly pulled Alex's hand back, but the baby must have found a comfortable position. After a minute, she let Alex go. "I guess the show is over."

"That was amazing. Thanks for sharing." Alex moved to the edge of the bed.

"Thank you for staying last night." Kimberly sat up.

Alex nodded. "I'd better go get dressed. Elle should be here in a few minutes."

The awkwardness that had dissipated during the baby's kicks returned full force as Alex walked out of the room.

ALEX HUNG HIS HEAD AND let the water run down his back. If only he could wash his emotions away as easily. Waking up next to Kimberly had easily been one of the most intimate moments of his life, and then to feel her baby move! If only he had a right to be there. If only she wanted him as her husband. Last night she'd been trying to get out of their marriage and not get either of them in legal trouble. If it became a real marriage, the insurance mess wouldn't be an issue.

Three weeks. Three weeks of laughing over meals. Misspelling words in Scrabble. Having her doze off in front of the TV using his shoulder as a pillow. Until last night, he'd kept telling himself it was part of the job, being friends, part of the territory.

It was a lie.

He'd known it was a lie the moment Uncle Donovan had called him into the conference room when Kimberly fainted and he'd wanted to whisk her out of there to someplace safe. At the time, he'd told himself it was because of the baby. Maybe even that it had to do with being jealous of his twin's marriage and pregnancy. But it was more.

Alex's phone beeped. It wasn't an urgent notification; nevertheless, Alex turned off the water and prepared to start the day pretending nothing had changed.

"Knock, knock."

Kimberly turned to the door. She had to look twice. Black was such a normal hair color. "Candace! When did you get back?"

"Late last night. That extra week we added to our vacation was wonderful. I came over as soon as I heard about your mother." Candace swooped in for a hug. "I thought you'd be getting ready to fly out there."

Kimberly shook her head. "It's a trap. My father-in-law will turn it into one if he hasn't already."

"But you have Alex and the FBI."

"Alex is part of the problem. So far, we've kept our marriage a secret from the media. I'm afraid if my father-in-law sees us together, he'll figure it out or someone will slip and call me Mrs. Hastings. The FBI uses that name, which I much prefer to Thompson, but then Alex would be in danger for the same reason I am, which I still don't understand. Jeremy hardly spoke to me. He didn't leave me any clues, and he didn't leave me a key. He didn't even leave me a will. Don't all rich people have wills?"

"I don't. Do you?" Candace pulled a chair up next to the one Kimberly sat on to paint.

"I'm working on one. The baby needs to be secure, and—" *Alex needs something.*

"And what?"

"Nothing."

Candace inspected Kimberly's drawing. "Does this big friendly bear have a name? He looks very kind and protective."

If only she'd maintained her habit of having two paintings so she could have hidden the bear the second Candace came in the room. "Not yet. He's a concept I've been working on."

"Hmmm. I think Zander would work very well for him. Those blue eyes remind me of the first bodyguard I ever met, Jethro Hastings. All his sons have them."

"Is it that obvious?"

"To anyone else? Probably not. But I've been listening to you say his name on the phone for almost a month. And seeing you say his name today and this drawing confirms it. He isn't just a bodyguard. What happened?"

Kimberly looked at the house. Somewhere, Elle sat observing. Kimberly put her fingers to her lips.

"I told Elle to take a walk. She isn't in there. And it's not likely anyone will get past Abbie's bodyguards. They even checked the trunk of my car before they let me in today. I've never seen them on such high alert."

"It's the triplets. Abbie is close to delivery, and every paparazzi on the planet is determined to scoop Preston's own magazines for the story. They even checked Elle's car." Kimberly moved inside to the more comfortable couches.

Candace moved a blue throw pillow and sat down. "See, she isn't here. Spill."

"He stayed with me last night."

Candace's penciled eyebrow rose.

"Oh, not like that. Get your head out of wherever. I mean after I got the call from the hospital. I must have called him. Or said his name and the phone did. Anyway, he came to my room, and I cried and cried. I was almost asleep when he started to leave. I begged him not to. I didn't want to be alone. I've been lonely for so long. And when Alex is near, I don't feel that emptiness. It was selfish, I know. This morning I woke up, and he was still there." Kimberly blinked back the tears. "I didn't want him to go, but he was already trying to leave. Then the baby kicked. Hard. It was as if she didn't want Alex to leave either, and we had this moment, the three of us. This was the moment I'd wished for the first time I was expecting, but I lost the baby, and Jeremy and I never got a chance. If Jeremy was alive, we probably wouldn't have had the chance to share this moment either. He was always working. I was only important when he needed me on his arm. Alex *sees* me. I don't think Jeremy ever did. I knew he didn't when we married, and I thought that was what I wanted."

"You're in love." There was no question in Candace's tone.

"Maybe. I don't know. What is love? I married Jeremy for his money. Mom always told me to marry for money since it lasts longer than love. And spare me the lecture. You were right. I figured our friendship would grow, but something happened when I lost our first baby and we moved to California. I never got our friendship back. I had thought we were starting to last fall"—Kimberly covered her belly—"or else I wouldn't have let this happen."

Candace rubbed Kimberly's shoulder. "To me, love is a guy who sees me without my hair or my prosthetics and thinks I'm beautiful and the adoring look in his eyes doesn't change, even when he sees the scars. It's messing with his computer system to lock him out of his inventions lab so we can talk for another hour and knowing he knew I changed the codes all along. It's watching him have a new idea and not minding I'll go to bed alone because when I wake up, he'll talk my head off about something that will save the world. It's wanting to be a better person because he exists."

"Is that all?"

"No. Love is the most amazing kisses I've ever known because I know he'll be there in the morning to kiss me again. It's finding a way to bring a two-centuries-old tradition back, even though I'm bald." The last words grew faint. Tears streamed down Candace's face.

Kimberly handed her the box of tissues and waited for the tears to subside. "What do you mean?"

"Colin found this journal by Emma Coons Wilson in a little museum in Massachusetts. She's my sixth great-grandmother. Every night, from her wedding night to the night he died, her husband Thomas brushed her hair one hundred strokes. She passed the tradition on to her daughters and her sons. There are some lines in the family that claim to still have the tradition. Obviously not a tradition I can use." Candace tugged at her black wig. "Brushing even my best wigs that much would ruin them. But every night, I lotion my scalp and, well, everything else. Colin's taken over the job, and since he can't do one hundred brush strokes, he calls it one hundred drops of lotion." The sappiness in Candace's grin could not be measured. "He even will come out of his invention room to do it. And you'll never believe what has been happening." She held her left arm at eye level.

Kimberly squinted. "Is that hair?"

"Yes! I told Colin if hair grows on my legs, I am not shaving for ten years, and he laughed."

"Love brought your hair back?"

"Maybe. I don't know. It doesn't matter to him if I have hair or not. That is what is important."

Kimberly gave Candace a hug. "I am so happy for you. Colin sounds perfect."

"He is, but marriage is hard work. Even with all the money in the world, we must work at it. So, what are you going to do to get things to work out with Alex?"

"I'm not."

"What?"

"It isn't fair to him. We married for the insurance, which is illegal, as his uncle pointed out. The best I can do is put the blame on me, pay the insurance company, and pray they don't prosecute him. His uncle is a deputy assistant director for the FBI, which spells DAD, which is weird. I know I'm wandering again. But I can't have Alex prosecuted for something he did so I could get an ultrasound. All because I didn't want to access my Leigh Benz account and trigger a search for me. Then it turned out only my accountant wouldn't have noticed anything for days anyway."

"You would have had to convince the county hospital you could use the Leigh Benz credit card and weren't stealing an identity. And that still could have alerted your father-in-law to where you were. Which is the reason you are living in the guesthouse of the Preston Harmon compound, which now may be the most secure place on earth other than Fort Knox and Area 51, with both Simon Dermot and Hastings Security guarding the place."

"But I made him lie. Integrity is everything to him. And I made Alex lie."

"What do you mean?"

"I don't know. Maybe something about loving and cherishing until death do we part? We both knew it was temporary. I lie to everyone. I live lies. I'm not even sure I know what my own truth is. It wasn't a big deal to me. But to a man like Alex? It must have crushed him." Kimberly wrung her hands. "I'm a terrible person. He deserves someone like him."

"Don't take this wrong, but I think part of this is your pregnancy hormones. Yes, you lie. But it is always for the good. Like when you broke my freshman glass and pretended it was yours. Or when you said you broke the skylight window again when it was really Carol's idiot boyfriend. I've never known you to lie about things that mattered."

"I told Jeremy I loved him. I lied."

"At the time, did you think you did?"

Kimberly shrugged. "I don't know. I loved what he represented, and I didn't mind being a trophy wife if it gave me security. I lived a lie. I lie about everything."

"Did you lie to the FBI?"

"No."

Candace raised a hand and counted off on her fingers. "Other than the glass, shrinking my favorite sweater, kissing the oboist when I was dating him—"

"You know about that?"

"—and claiming you lost your key when you hid it under a rock so you could get a spare, have you ever lied to me?"

"Does pretending I was sick and skipping class count?"

"Freshman English? Definitely not. That grad student was an idiot."

"Then, no." Kimberly hugged Candace. "But I lied when I took my vows and married Alex."

"Then you can either come clean or make them real."

What if making them real forces Alex to lie more? "And that is my problem."

THE PHONE RANG AS ALEX sat in his office going over plans to improve security at Ogilvie Tower.

"This is Mr. Alexander."

Uncle Donovan's voice boomed over the line. "Hey, Alex, this is a courtesy call. Agents Danes and Garcia are coming in on the 11:00 a.m. flight. They want to escort your wife back to California for the funeral. They are sure Kimberly has access to something that will be the key to the case."

"She doesn't want to go. Can they force her to?"

"They can creatively coerce her."

The urge to growl like a caveman swelled in his chest. "Do they know where she is?"

"Not yet. I'd like to keep Abbie out of this. Can you get Kimberly to the office at one?"

"I'll try."

"Thanks."

Alex closed his computer. On the way out, he stopped by his father's office. "The FBI wants Kimberly to fly out to California. If she goes, I'd like a four-person team, including Elle. Who can you spare?"

"Adam and September got back from her tour the other night. Take Adam. He needs a short-term job. Alan will be useless to me if you take Elle, but he will be useless to you if you take him, so either take Andrew if he is over his jet lag or someone off the Crawford team. Mrs. Crawford cleared her schedule for the next few days, saying little Joy needed some quiet time after the vacation."

A four-week trip with a one-year-old? Even with a nanny, everyone probably needed quiet time. "Thanks. I'll give Adam and Andrew a call as soon as I know anything. Will you keep Alan from calling Elle every twenty minutes?"

"He isn't that bad, is he?"

"No, but Elle is inside of the Harmon compound most of the day and he still worries."

Jethro laughed. "How did I get four hardheaded sons?"

"Four?"

"Yes, I am including you. Go on now."

"Bye, Dad. And I am not hardheaded."

Mrs. Ogilvie's car sat in front of the guest cottage. Alex checked his app. She'd been here well over an hour. How had he missed her visit? He wasn't directly over Mrs. Ogilvie's security, but it should have registered she was with Kimberly. Elle came around the side of the house.

"Hi, Mr. Alexander."

"Perimeter walks?"

"Mrs. Ogilvie asked me to make myself scarce. They are both in the living room, and no one other than me has come near the house. Is something wrong?"

"Maybe. I will take over for now. I need you to get your go-bag ready. Make sure you have two suits, a dress suitable for a funeral, and some casual wear. We may go to California, and having you blend in may work better than having you look like a bodyguard."

Elle beamed. "Alan is okay with this?"

"Jethro is. Also, call Adam and Andrew and ask them to pack their four-day bags and to have those and some shorts ready for California. If Andrew sounds like he has any jet lag, call someone from Ben's team."

"You trust me to choose?"

"You know every employee we have. I know you'll make a good choice."

"Will do." Elle trotted to her car.

Alex made as much noise as possible entering the house. "Mrs. Ogilvie, I didn't expect to see you here. How was your trip?"

"How long is it going to take before you call me Candace again?" Candace rolled her eyes.

"You are a client."

"I know you call all your clients by their titles except for Mrs. Thompson—I mean Hastings."

"Correct. I call Kimberly by her name because it seems like the best thing to call her."

"You called me Candace for two years before you started the Mrs. Ogilvie stuff. Come on, Alex."

Alex rubbed the back of his neck. He didn't need this right now. "Fine. Hello, Candace. How are you?"

"Just peachy. However, I need to run." Candace hugged Kimberly and whispered something in her ear.

Kimberly turned an adorable shade of pink.

"I'll see you two later." Candace closed the front door behind her. Her car started, and she drove past the window.

"Doesn't Candace have a bodyguard with her?" asked Kimberly.

"One followed her here and stayed outside the gate. Candace won't give up driving."

"Oh. Do I want to know what serious business brought you here in the middle of the day?"

Alex took the seat Candace had vacated. "Probably not."

145

"Oh, then you better tell me fast."

"Agents Danes and Garcia are flying into O'Hare and should be here in an hour."

"Let me guess—they want me to attend the memorial service so they can follow me around and see if I know anything."

"Pretty much."

Kimberly crossed her arms. "I don't want to go. I knew Mom could pass while I was gone, and I said my goodbyes. Whoever killed Jeremy and the other FBI agent is out there, and if the FBI and my father-in-law think I know something or have something I don't, it will only put everyone in danger. What is to stop them from killing me too?"

"Me."

"No. Alex, you can't put your life on the line for me."

"Last time I checked my job description, that was pretty much it."

Kimberly buried her head in her hands. Alex laid a hand on her back, resisting the urge to pull her into his lap. "I'll bring the best team with me, plus you'll have the FBI. I'll ask Preston if we can use his plane. You'll have a private bedroom."

Kimberly looked up. "Seriously? Preston's plane has a bedroom?"

"And the most amazing reclining leather seats. I am 100 percent sure he has no plans to use it for the next several weeks. He started working from home today to be near Abbie." Alex slid his hand down Kimberly's arm to her hand. "Before we go anywhere, we will check with Dr. Song. If she doesn't clear you to fly, it doesn't matter if the FBI provides a legion of agents. You won't go."

"If I can go, I don't want the FBI on the plane. They don't deserve reclining leather seats."

Alex pulled Kimberly into a side hug. "Agreed. We've been asked to meet them at the FBI field office at one."

"Should I pack first?"

"Call Dr. Song first. All of their arguments will be worthless if it isn't safe for you to fly."

Alex went to pack his bag while Kimberly was on the phone. That way she could give him any answer she wanted to.

A moment later, she tapped on his door. "Dr. Song says I should be good to fly since I'm in my thirty-second week and I haven't had any more spotting. She asked me to have Abbie's nurse-midwife check my blood pressure and stuff first. Do you want to walk up with me?"

"Anytime."

"Good, you can carry anything I borrow from Abbie."

"And here I thought you were getting used to having a bodyguard follow you around. You just wanted me for my muscles."

THE PLANE WAS MORE AMAZING than she imagined. Agents Danes and Garcia already had return flight tickets and flew commercial back to California. Danes clearly wished to fly with Kimberly, but Agent Garcia found wisdom in flying separately. They asked that Kimberly's flight land after theirs so they could meet it, but Alex informed them Kimberly wouldn't fly out until the next morning. She suspected it was as much for her as it was for his youngest brother, who had returned from Europe.

Sunlight glistened off the Great Lakes below them as the pilot banked the plane into the turn that would set them on course for California. At the front of the cabin, Alex conferred with Elle and his brothers. Kimberly touched the empty seat next to her, hoping Alex would fill it before the flight was over. Then again, it might be for the best if he didn't.

Last night, he'd hugged her after they watched a rerun of some black-and-white comedy. Then he'd offered to stay with her if she didn't want to be alone. Saying no had been difficult. She'd regretted it almost every hour of the night as she tossed and turned. Knowing it wasn't fair to him was the only thing that had kept her from crying his name in the dark hours of the morning, knowing he would come.

Kimberly reclined her seat and let the hum of the plane lull her into sleep.

She half heard, half felt Alex take the seat beside her. He touched her arm. "Kimberly?"

She opened an eye with some effort.

"Do you want to try the bed? You might sleep better."

No, I'll sleep better here if you stay beside me. "I'm fine here."

"You sure?"

Kimberly leaned her head against his arm and nodded.

Adam shook Alex's shoulder. "Half hour till touchdown."

Alex nodded. Kimberly still slept on his shoulder. He trailed a finger down her face. "Kimberly?"

She opened her eyes and closed them again.

"Time to wake up. Half hour till we land. You can use the restroom."

Kimberly's eyes opened. "You shouldn't say that word. The baby knows what it means and starts dancing on my kidneys." She unbuckled her seat belt.

Alex got out of his seat. "There is a bathroom through the bedroom. Your bags are in the closet in case you want to change or anything."

Kimberly smoothed her navy-blue maternity dress. "Do I need to change?"

Alex ran a knuckle along her cheek. "No, but you are wearing the wrinkles of my shirt on your face."

Kimberly rubbed her face and walked to the back of the plane. Alex watched her go.

"Just what part of your marriage isn't real?" asked Adam in his ear. "I may be only almost-engaged, but yours seems like it could be the real thing to me."

Alex turned to his brother. "If wishes were fishes."

"I prefer 'if wishes were kisses.'" Adam stepped back, grinning.

"Neither one will help me, so let it go."

"You should talk about it with her. September and I could have saved ourselves so much pain if we had talked things out a year ago."

"As long as I am Kimberly's bodyguard and we are possibly committing fraud, I don't know that we can talk things out."

"Point taken. Mrs. Ogilvie is paying you to be her husband. That is awkward." Adam laughed.

Worse, Kimberly would pay Mrs. Ogilvie back, making him ... Alex closed his eyes and counted to five. "Adam, back off."

Adam nodded, made a point of looking over Alex's shoulder, and returned to the front of the plane.

"Something wrong?" asked Kimberly from behind him.

"Nothing more than brotherly love." Alex stood so Kimberly could get back in her seat, then lowered himself back into his. "Ready for this?"

"The landing or being on edge for the next seventy-two hours?"

"Both?"

"Neither." She gripped his hands. "I've never been afraid of landings, but I had some very bumpy ones the last few times I flew, and I always worried the baby might get hurt."

"I think your child has the most comfortable seat in the house."

"I'm not too sure. This chair is nice." She snuggled into his side.

The pilot's voice came over the intercom advising them to check their seat belts. Alex looked to make sure Kimberly's was secure.

She patted his hand. "Don't worry. I'm safe."

He was glad she thought so.

Three government-issue SUVs waited at the end of the tarmac. Alex looped Kimberly's arm through his.

Agent Danes came forward to meet them. "Mrs. Hastings."

Alex stopped short. They had discussed this less than twenty-four hours ago. "Remember, it is Mrs. Thompson or Kimberly while we are here."

"Then you might want to act more like a bodyguard and less like a husband." Agent Garcia joined them.

Kimberly slipped her arm out of his. "Mr. Alexander was helping me cross the tarmac." She raised her chin. "What is first on your agenda for me?"

"We would like you to look around your house. I'll go with you in plain clothes, along with her." Agent Garcia pointed to Elle. "It will look like we are just three friends."

Adam looked at Alex over Elle's head. The numbers weren't good—two armed women and Kimberly against any number of bodyguards. "Don't you have a warrant?"

"The judge doesn't feel we have enough evidence for one. Most of our evidence is from what Jeremy gave us." Agent Danes crossed his arms.

"Do you know how many guards are at the house? There used to be three plus the staff. There was a reason I eluded them and disappeared. I don't think the three of us are safe. My father-in-law will be notified the moment I try to enter. Do you really think he will let me leave? After all, he owns the house."

"What?" asked the agents.

"Don't tell me you didn't know that? I didn't know it until after Jeremy died. I'd assumed it was his. Hawthorn pointed out that he didn't have to let me live there at least a dozen times and showed me the deed. I thought your accountants would have known that by now." Kimberly crossed her arms.

Agent Danes stepped forward. "You aren't willing to go in? You said you would yesterday."

Alex tried to step between Danes and Kimberly, but Kimberly nudged him out of the way. "Yesterday, I thought we would all be going in. My four trusted bodyguards and you. I'll try it, but only if they are all included."

Agent Garcia frowned. "I guess they could pass for some concerned cousins. Very buff concerned cousins."

"Maybe. Check the feed from Mrs. Ha—Thompson's press conference. If Mr. Hastings is in the background, that might not work." Agent Danes gave the command to one of the other FBI agents standing near the cars.

Alex prayed his face wasn't on the screen.

The rental minivan smelled like cheap pine air-freshener and stale cheese curds. Only Kimberly noticed. "Pregnancy nose" was what Elle called it. Andrew drove. Unfortunately, Alex could be seen in one of the cable news feeds, and Adam looked too much like Alex, but Andrew's darker wavy hair and five-o'clock shadow set him apart from his brothers enough that Agent Danes agreed he could go. Agents Danes and Garcia sat in the second-row captain's chairs, Elle and another agent in the back seat. They'd practiced emptying the van in an airport hangar until both Danes and Alex were satisfied Kimberly could be protected in an emergency.

Kimberly adjusted her maternity blouse where it had gotten stuck on the protective vest absolutely everyone insisted she wear, necessitating a change of clothing. At only six pounds, it was lighter than she thought it would be, though far from being a comfortable fit. Elle tried to console her by pointing out they weren't exactly comfortable on a nonpregnant body either.

At the last turn, the SUV behind them pulled over. Kimberly tried to catch a glimpse of Alex through the side mirror, but the windows were too dark.

Andrew turned into the drive of Kimberly's old house, stopped at the closed gate, then rolled down his window and punched in the code Kimberly gave him. The driveway gate didn't open, but the smaller sidewalk gate did. Jax and another bodyguard came out.

Jax approached the driver's-side window. "Mrs. Thompson. So nice to see you. Unfortunately, I have orders not to allow you in. Especially with so many friends."

"Jax, I'm here for my mother's funeral. All I want is a photo and some memorabilia. Please let me in."

"Who are all your friends? I was unaware you had so many." Jax leaned into Andrew's window.

Kimberly assumed he was stalling for time. It would take her father-in-law at least seven minutes to get to the gate if he was home. Longer if he was farther. "This is Drew. He is Elle's brother. Elle, wave at Jax." Elle waved from the back seat. "Elle and I are staying in the same house. Over there is her boyfriend, Alan." Since it was easier to keep the lie closest to the truth, Kimberly called the agent whose name she'd forgotten by Alan Hastings's name. "Elle's never been to California. I told her we could see the beach and the Golden Gate after the funeral. Then my friend Maria and her husband, Danes. Andrew came along to even out the numbers and to drive. As you know, I've never been fond of driving in California traffic."

Jax turned his attention to Andrew. "Do you like to drive?"

"Sure. Your traffic isn't as bad as Chicago's. I spend a lot of my time driving. I have an Illinois chauffeur's license. Would you like to see it?" Andrew reached for his wallet.

Jax held up a hand. "No need."

A car pulled crossways behind them. Hawthorn Thompson got out and came to the passenger-side door.

Kimberly rolled her window halfway down.

"Kimberly, dear, we've missed you so. Are you back to stay?" Her father-in-law stood on tiptoe to peer into the back of the van.

"No. I came to get a few photos of Mom for the funeral tomorrow and a few mementos. Jax says I can't go in my house."

"Kimberly, I've explained this before. This isn't your house; it's mine. I was letting you and Jeremy use it. I offered to let you stay. But since you said I was abusive, I don't think I should let you in."

"I recall more threats that I would have to leave if I didn't produce items of Jeremy's that I don't have." Kimberly needed to get him talking.

"It's only natural that I want some of my son's belongings."

"Is that why you had people search the house and install cameras?"

"I needed to find some things Jeremy had. The cameras were for your protection."

"Really? You needed to protect me in the studio, my bedroom, and my bathroom? Without my knowledge? That's not protection—that's voyeurism." Kimberly spat the word.

"But what if you fell in the shower?"

"You did? You had one in my bathroom?"

A lecherous grin grew on his face.

No! Kimberly struggled to hide her shock and keep her breakfast down. She'd never found a camera in the bathroom or bedroom, only the studio. The bathroom had been a guess. "There was always a maid or two or a bodyguard around to hear me scream."

"Let's not talk about that in front of your friends. Come inside with me, and we can find your photos."

"My friends are coming with me. I will not be alone with a father-in-law who's admitted he watched me in the shower."

"Kimberly, Kimberly." Hawthorn Thompson shook his head and wrapped his hand around the half-open window. "There you go again, being hysterical over nothing. I never said I watched you in the shower. I worried about you falling. After losing three, or was it four, babies, I wanted to make sure nothing happened to this grandchild, my legacy."

Bile rose in Kimberly's throat. The image of opening the door and tossing up her accounts on her father-in-law's shoes was very satisfying. But opening the door could put them all in danger.

Kimberly took a deep breath. "So, what you are saying is I can only get my mother's photo if I go with you alone?"

"If it would make you feel better, one of your little girlfriends can come too, but then Jax would need to be with us in case she has sticky fingers." Kimberly looked at Agent Garcia, who tapped her fingers twice. No. "What if I tell you where the photo is and Jax goes in and gets it?"

"Sorry, Jax is security, not a gofer."

"Then I guess I must hold the funeral without the photo." Kimberly pushed the button to roll up the window.

"Wait!" Hawthorn held on to the window with enough force to keep it from going up. "Do you realize your $25 million could have saved my son's life? If you'd let him invest it with me, he'd still be alive. What will the tabloids do with the story I have to tell? The children's author who let her husband die."

"That's not true!" How could he say that? Jeremy told her not to invest with them.

"Yes, it is. Maybe Jeremy didn't know what your little hobby was. Maybe that is why you are so good at keeping secrets. Give me what he left you, and I'll leave you alone."

Kimberly covered her mouth and closed her eyes. She needed to give the signal to leave but couldn't.

"Hold!" shouted Andrew as he revved the van's motor.

Agent Danes gripped Kimberly's shoulders as they'd practiced in the event they needed to make a fast vehicular exit. As the van jerked and turned around, Kimberly opened her eyes and used her free hand to grab her armrest. The back of the van collided with her father-in-law's BMW, pushing it out into the street. Andrew quickly moved from reverse into forward. Kimberly's head jerked, and she swallowed the bile in her throat.

ALEX FISTED HIS HANDS. THE FBI driver activated his lights and waited for the van to come out of the lane before taking off after it. A separate FBI vehicle turned into the lane to block any cars in pursuit.

Andrew's voice came over the listening equipment. "We need a closer rendezvous. Am I clear for the strip mall on the left or the park behind it?"

The technician behind Alex answered. "Pull into the strip mall. With the damage to the back of the van, we can cover it as a traffic stop. Make for the largest clear space you can."

"Will do."

"Two and three, meet us at the new location. Dispatch, arrange for a tow truck to pick up the van. I'll send the address as soon as we stop."

Alex watched Andrew park the van near the end of a vacant row of cars, their SUV pulling up beside it. Alex flung his door open before anyone could stop him and ran to the passenger side of the van. Kimberly had the door open and was leaning over the pavement. He stopped just in time to avoid getting vomit on his shoes and pants. The sliding door behind her opened, Agent Danes making a disgusted face as he exited.

Alex reached for Kimberly. "Are you finished?"

Kimberly didn't answer but gripped his hand.

Elle exited the van and thrust a wipe into his hand. Alex handed it to Kimberly, and she wiped her face off. "I think I'm done."

Alex studied the bilious puddle. "Sit back for a moment." Carefully placing his feet on either side of the mess, he eased Kimberly back into the passenger seat.

Andrew still sat at the wheel. "Shall I pull forward?"

Alex stepped back and held on to the open door. "Four feet will do."

The van rolled forward. The second it stopped, Alex reached for Kimberly.

She threw her arms around him. "I didn't know. I wondered, but I didn't know. It is so sick."

Alex shifted Kimberly, lifted her out of the van, and set her on her feet. He pushed the anger at Hawthorn away and tried to comfort his wife.

"I didn't know." She tried to shake him.

Elle stood by, holding out an uncapped water bottle. "Kimberly, rinse your mouth."

Kimberly took a drink, and Elle held out another wipe. Alex wondered if they'd done this before.

"Don't think I'll ever get that taste out of my mouth. My father-in-law watched me. I looked for a camera, but it was hard without being obvious. I stumbled upon the one in the studio, and I realized there had to be others, but my bathroom—that's just sick." Kimberly took another drink.

Agent Garcia approached. "We'd like to leave here as soon as possible. Kimberly and Alex, if you'll get in that vehicle over there, we'll debrief elsewhere."

Alex helped Kimberly into the SUV. A thin sheen of perspiration coated her brow. "Do you need another minute?"

Kimberly shook her head. "Just aim the AC at my face."

As Alex rounded the vehicle, Agent Danes stopped him. "Please don't let her do that again."

"You mean confront her father-in-law? Not my call. If you are talking about losing her breakfast, I think all of us wanted to do that listening to him. Believe me, she didn't enjoy the experience either." Alex pushed past the agent and into the SUV.

Agent Danes got into the driver's seat.

"Agents I need to go to the hotel now." Kimberly's face had lost all color her voice was barely a whisper.

Agent Garcia turned in her seat. "We've arranged a safe house."

"Hastings Security has also arranged a safe place for me. And right now, I prefer to be there." Her voice was more firm.

The agents looked at each other.

Alex spoke up. "That was our agreement yesterday. It is obvious Kimberly needs rest. If you'll take us back to the airstrip, we'll escort her from there."

Agent Danes nodded to Agent Garcia.

Alex reached for Kimberly's hand.

The luxury house was far from the hotel Kimberly had pictured, her feet sinking into the soft carpet of the white-on-white living room. "How did you find this?"

Adam set two suitcases down inside the front door. "It's a property September used on her music tour last month. It's owned by a reputable firm that rents houses to celebrities and such. It comes with a full security package and five bedrooms. The gated community adds an extra layer of security. Too bad we probably won't use it again."

"Why not?" asked Elle.

"Everything is white on white or seafoam blue. Harmony is beginning to crawl, and the potential for messes stressed September out. She is thinking next tour she wants to get two tour buses and live out of them. Hopefully, we will be married by then. This was only a short tour, but Harmony made switching hotels and flying more complicated than we expected. We were both glad it was a six-week tour."

Kimberly had only briefly met the singer Adam had proposed to. "I liked her song about postpartum depression. Because of it and because every magazine on earth has been carrying articles about postpartum depression, I feel like I am better prepared to recognize it if I get it. When are you two getting married?"

"Still to be determined. September wants to be sure she is not thinking with her hormones or anything. Back in our grandparents' day, they might say we were pinned, or had plans to be engaged. She's officially my girl and will probably say yes to my proposal, but—" Adam shrugged. "We don't have a date yet."

"Oh."

Andrew and Alex came in with the last of the bags. "Did anyone decide rooms?"

They all looked to Adam.

"The upstairs suite in the back has a great ocean view. Kimberly should have it as it can't be seen from the road. Elle and Alex, take the two rooms across the hall. Andrew and I can take the downstairs rooms. Does that work for everyone? The kitchen should be stocked with sandwich things, basic breakfast items, and fruit and vegetables."

Kimberly started up the stairs with her small duffel, knowing Alex would bring her suitcase. The large suite featured a wall of french doors and windows looking out on the bay. Kimberly opened the door and let the sea breeze wash over her. The smell of sea salt tingled. Seagulls squawked high above waves that crashed against the rocky shoreline. Natures best white noise.

"Here's your suitcase."

Kimberly beckoned Alex closer. "This is gorgeous. Perfect. I can't thank you guys enough for not stuffing me into some hotel room or whatever safe house the FBI had in mind."

"Adam said it was peaceful, and even though it's a few miles farther from the church and cemetery than we were hoping, I thought peaceful trumped a bit of inconvenience."

"I agree. I hope the FBI releases my funds so I can pay for this."

Alex held up a hand. "You get to fight payment out with Mrs. Og—I mean Candace."

"It really is hard for you to use her name, isn't it?"

"Yes. I need to distance myself from my clients."

"So our situation must be difficult."

Alex nodded. "Do you need a snack before you take a nap?"

"I'd better. Yogurt, if they have some. I'm not very hungry."

When Alex left, Kimberly pulled a maternity T-shirt Abbie had given her with the words *Tired, Hungry,* and *Blessed* across the front and a pair of basketball shorts from her suitcase. By the time Alex returned, she'd settled into a double chaise lounge in the deck's shade.

Alex placed a water bottle and a vanilla Greek yogurt with berries and granola on the table next to her.

Kimberly patted the space next to her. "Stay? I don't want to be alone with my thoughts."

"Do you want to talk about anything?"

"Anything that has nothing to do with my father-in-law."

"How about I tell you the story of the Hastings boys' raft that didn't make it across Lake Michigan to Canada?"

Kimberly picked up her yogurt. "I'm all ears."

The chaise lounge was still in the shade when Elle woke Alex with a tap on his shoulder. Elle pointed downstairs and then at herself and a nearby chair. Alex pointed to a pillow, which Elle handed him; he used it to replace his shoulder as he rolled away from Kimberly's side.

Alex found his brothers sitting at the kitchen table, a phone between them. "Agent Danes called. He says if Kimberly will agree to file charges for voyeurism, they can hold Hawthorn Thompson for two days. In California, voyeurism is only a misdemeanor, lumped under a statute for invasion of privacy. It isn't much, but it will give the FBI access to the house and hopefully add more charges."

"That's stupid," said Alex.

"True. But they can put him in jail for twenty-four hours and get a warrant to search both houses. If the video feed also went to the bodyguards or anywhere else, they could add distribution of the material, which carries a stiffer sentence. Depending on how many days they filmed Kimberly, they may be facing multiple charges."

Alex pushed back from the table. "I don't even want to think about what they filmed. You saw her this morning. She asked me not to leave so she could take a nap. I told her the most embellished version of our raft story ever to get her to relax. Adam, you should have hero complex."

"I get it. It nearly killed me when I learned what September's agent had done. But I had to let September choose what to do and pray it would all work out," said Adam. "This needs to be Kimberly's choice."

"They'll pick him up today, so he won't be at the funeral?"

Andrew nodded. "Yes. Agent Danes said they'd work with the local police on that."

"I get to break the news to Kimberly?"

"You seem to be the best man for the job," said Adam. "She'll have to go into the field office. The agents think they can do everything from there and not have to go to the police station too."

"For the record, I don't like this." Alex walked slowly up the stairs.

Kimberly signed the statement and pushed it across the table to Agent Garcia and a police detective whose name had been mentioned multiple times but refused to stay in her memory. "Is that all?"

The detective picked up the paper. "That is all I need. I got a text from my partner. It looks like the hit-and-run reported this morning in front of your old house was a clear case of self-defense. Since the FBI reported it first, we are putting the circumstances on the report for the insurance companies."

Kimberly could hear Alex responding to them, but she couldn't focus on what he was saying—she just wanted out of the little interview room. Away from questions she didn't have answers for. Away from the assumptions of what recordings were hiding on her father-in-law's computer. Away from the men who might review those recordings.

Alex helped her up and put an arm around her. In the elevator, she leaned her head against his chest to block everything out. Alex placed a protective hand on her back. When the elevator stopped, he got her to the car. If the brothers were talking, she didn't hear them.

Elle forced an open water bottle into her hand. "I think we should go find some ice cream. We haven't had any since Monday."

Kimberly nodded. Ice cream equaled brain freeze, and brain freeze was better than wondering how long the cameras had been there or if Jeremy ever suspected if the cameras had anything to do with him choosing to sleep in separate rooms.

The car started. As Alex held her hand and rubbed the back of it with his thumb, Kimberly focused on the warmth radiating from his touch and the computer voice telling Andrew to turn left in one thousand feet, then right in a quarter mile.

She didn't want to know.

She didn't want to testify.

She also didn't want her father-in-law walking free.

Mostly Kimberly didn't want to feel the cacophony of emotions rushing through her. Yet she couldn't find anything else to focus on. Andrew parked the SUV. Elle spoke and Kimberly nodded, and Alex placed an ice cream cone in her hand, but the brain freeze wasn't intense or quick enough. Gradually the soft stream of voices flowed around her, warm and caring. Alex had his hand on her back, and Andrew was telling some lame computer joke. Kimberly smiled, not at the punch line but at everyone's reactions to the joke. She found Alex's hand and a safe anchor.

Rocky Road. She half completed the cone before the flavor registered. Kimberly looked at Elle and Alex, wondering who'd ordered for her. Alex of course.

"Anyone up for finding a beach?" Elle grinned, a smudge of blue ice cream clinging to her lip.

"You've really never been to the beach?" asked Andrew. "I thought it was just a story."

"Never."

Alex moved his thumb across Kimberly's spine, a gentle nudge indicating that the choice was hers.

"I'd like to go if we can find one that isn't too crowded."

Andrew and Alan consulted the maps on their phones.

Kimberly turned enough to look at Alex. "It's still Wednesday, right?"

Popping the last of his cone in his mouth, Alex nodded.

"There should be a Bible study at my old church tonight at seven. Can we go?"

"I don't see why not. Will it look weird to have us with you?"

"Jax's crew used to follow me. They'd stand by the wall and glare."

"I'll probably sit with you and participate. It's been awhile since I've been to Bible study. Elle will too. Adam and Alan will be the more formal presence if needed, or they can blend in. Do you know what they are studying?"

Kimberly pulled up the search engine on her phone. "It should be on the website."

"Do they have a building floor plan on there too?"

Kimberly handed him the phone and returned to finishing her cone.

Alex handed her phone to Adam to make the final decision.

"We're good for Bible study."

Kimberly laughed. "I'm glad to know you'll be 'good' for it. I'd have to explain if you were bad."

Alex laughed. The others joined in.

Soon they were back in the vehicle and headed for the beach. As the sun warmed Kimberly through the window, she knew she could survive this day too.

PAYING MORE ATTENTION TO KIMBERLY than the Bible app
on his phone, Alex missed it when they changed chapters. He
scrambled to find the new verse before anyone could ask him to
read. Two older women sized him up with disapproving glares.

The discussion leader finished with the chapter and closed her
Bible. "I know we have all been eager to say something since
Kimberly and her friends snuck in here late, but let me be the
first to welcome you. And I am sorry about your mother."

The women swarmed Kimberly with hugs and condolences.
A few even touched her belly. The last of the strain drained out of
Kimberly's face as an elderly woman pressed a kiss to her cheek.

Alex stepped to one side, Elle to the other. Adam and Alex
were somewhere else in the building, keeping watch.

A short, pink-haired woman in her seventies approached Alex.
"Are you another one of those bodyguards or a boyfriend? You
look like you could take down that no-good bodyguard who used
to follow her to church. But when I see you looking at my little
Kimberly... well, it gets me to wondering what your intentions
are."

"I'm a man who will protect Kimberly and her child with my
life." Alex hoped it was a satisfactory answer.

The woman stuck out a hand. "Gladys. Nice to meet you. Are you in town for the funeral?"

"Yes, ma'am."

"Good. Promise to keep her as far from her no-good father-in-law as you can. He and the media twisted Pastor Baxter's words for the news report, making it sound like we doubted her when we were cheering her on. Some of us even called in false leads. I said I saw her get off a plane in Fairbanks."

Alex smiled and wondered how the church-going woman had dealt with the lie.

Kimberly exchanged greetings with a woman about her age in pink scrubs. Alex couldn't hear what was being said but as concerned faces relaxed, he did too. Elle moved closer to the door—a better position to watch the entire room.

Gladys spoke loudly to a woman near her age. "Boyfriend. Lynda, see how he can't keep his eyes off her? Wonder if he can stay for some of your lemon bars."

"I can." Alex made a show of looking around the room for the treats.

Both women laughed. "The refreshments are in the fellow-ship hall."

Alex nodded and moved to Kimberly's side. A middle-aged woman was giving her a hug. "I have something for you. It came in the mail last week. I put it in your cubby in the nursery so I wouldn't forget it."

"Letter?"

"It says 'Happy birthday' on the outside."

Alex panicked. He hadn't missed her birthday, had he? No, it was still a month away. He'd made a note of it when they applied for the wedding license.

Kimberly cocked her head. "That's odd. My birthday is still weeks away. I'll get it before I leave. Thank you, Tammy."

"After the funeral, you're going back to—?"

Kimberly patted Alex's arm. "I'm going back to a safe place."

Gladys craned her head back to take in all of Alex. "He does look like a safe place. Oh, look. Everybody is leaving. We better hurry if we want one of Lynda's lemon bars."

"They're the best." Kimberly reached for Alex's hand but stopped before her fingers touched his and turned the motion into a "Follow me."

Alex touched Kimberly's elbow. "Letter or lemon bars first?"

"Letter?"

The children's drawings on the wall had changed since the last time she'd been there. Instead of Easter lilies, flags now covered the tackboards. Alex and Elle followed Kimberly to the cupboard at one end of the room, where she opened the doors to reveal rows of shelves divided into sections. As she reached for a cubbyhole above her head, Alex caught her hand. "Don't touch it."

"Do you have any gallon-sized bags around?" asked Elle.

Kimberly dropped her hand and went over to another cupboard, where she unlatched a child-safe lock. "We have gallon, half gallon, sandwich, and quart." She moved a box. "And two-gallon."

"Zipper bags?" Elle joined her.

"All but the sandwich bags."

Elle poked around in the cupboard. "Would they mind if we took a two-gallon bag and this plastic knife?"

"I don't think so."

Elle stuffed the knife into her back pocket, then turned the bag inside out, creating a huge plastic mitten. She stood on tiptoes to see into Kimberly's space, then stepped back, handing the bag to Alex. "You're the tall one. Perhaps you should do the honors."

Alex took the bag as Elle had and used it to retrieve the bright-yellow, oversized envelope from the cubby. He used his free hand to pull the bag over the card.

"Don't close it yet." Elle dropped the plastic knife into the bag, then sealed the bag. Alex raised a brow. Elle rolled her eyes. "I'll show you later. Let's go get one of those lemon bars." Elle tucked the bag holding the card into her purse.

"Don't I get to see it?"

Alex put a hand on Kimberly's back. "Later. It may not be something you want to read here. Which way to the fellowship hall?"

Kimberly frowned, but he was right. The last thing she needed was to break down with all her friends around. People milled around the fellowship hall with glasses of lemonade or water and small plates of cookies. Pastor Baxter hurried across the room when he saw them.

"Kimberly, I am so glad you came tonight. It surprised me you changed your mind about the celebration-of-life service for your mother."

"I was too, but I needed to come back."

"I am glad you did. I've wanted to talk to you ever since the interview aired. I always heard the media could twist someone's words through editing, but I didn't believe it until I saw what they did to mine."

Kimberly gave the pastor a half smile. "When I first heard it, it upset me. However, I had a friend point out that what I heard might not be what you said. I haven't thought about it since."

The pastor gave Kimberly's baby bump a significant look. "It looks like you've had other things on your mind."

Kimberly placed a protective hand on her belly. "Yes, among other things. Do you have a moment we could talk in private?" The question surprised her as much as it seemed to surprise Alex, who dropped his hand from her back.

"In my office."

Kimberly looked at Alex before answering. His face remained passive. Since it wasn't a no, Kimberly said, "Yes, please."

The pastor led the way to the small office at the end of another hallway. Alex and Elle remained outside. Pastor Baxter showed Kimberly a seat. "I see you have a new set of body-guards. Much nicer than your old ones. Oh, before I forget—here is the key to the storage unit I moved your mother's worldly belongings to."

Kimberly took the key, and the pastor sat down on his side of the desk. "What is troubling you?"

"I'm married."

"Well, technically not anymore. Jeremy is dead."

"No, I married Alex Hastings four weeks ago under false pre-tenses, and I don't know what to do."

"If there is fraud, you can annul it."

"That is part of the problem. Even though neither of us thought about it at the time, we got married so I would have insurance and could get an ultrasound to make sure the baby was safe. And that is insurance fraud."

"Oh, fraud is a complication. I suppose as well as an annulment you would need to pay a fine or something."

"What if that something is jail? I don't want to lose my baby."

The pastor leaned back in his chair and steepled his fingers under his nose. "Definitely a problem."

They sat in silence for a moment.

Pastor Baxter opened his bible. "Have you ever considered Adam and Eve?"

"I have."

"Did you realize they were the first arranged marriage?"

Kimberly thought about it for a moment. "I've never thought about them as an arranged marriage."

"For thousands of years, people have arranged millions of mar-riages among all cultures of the world. The two of you might not have married for the traditional reasons, but if you choose to work on your marriage as Adam and Eve must have, the insur-ance fraud goes away, doesn't it?"

"But what if it doesn't work out? I can't live in another failing marriage like I did with Jeremy."

"How hard did you try to make the marriage with Jeremy work? And I'm not talking the last few months before his death. I am referring to day one, day two, and so forth. How much effort did you put into your relationship?"

Kimberly squirmed in her seat. "Not very much."

"The Bible doesn't tell us much about Adam and Eve, but they didn't have very many options. Who else could they have married? Divorce hadn't been invented. I am sure they had rough times. Eve burned the stew, and Adam brought home a pheasant hardly big enough to feed themselves, let alone the boys who had been fighting all day as only Cain and Abel could. Yet they made it work. So you didn't marry Alex under ideal circumstances. What do you know of him? Does he treat you with respect?"

Kimberly nodded.

"Could he be a good father to your child?"

Again, she nodded.

"Do you respect him?"

"Yes."

"I saw him in Bible study with you. He seemed to know his way around the scriptures. You both share your faith. You can build on that and learn to pray together. It may be cliché, but in my years here, I have found that couples who pray together stay together."

Kimberly nodded.

Pastor Baxter looked at his watch. "I should let you go. One more thought. I've done my share of counseling over the years and seen couples fall in love. The only ones who make it are the ones who are committed and who work to make it happen. Love isn't meant to be easy."

Kimberly stood and shook the pastor's hand. "You've given me a lot to think about."

He didn't release her hand. "I assume you haven't consummated your marriage."

Heat rose in her face. "No, I'm under doctor's orders…"

"Until you are committed, I strongly suggest you don't. The

state doesn't care about that anymore as far as annulments are concerned, but avoiding deep intimacy will make it easier to remain friends if you choose not to make the marriage work."

Kimberly exited the room, her simple question multiplying into more complicated ones.

The GPS instructions were the only noise on the ride back to the rental house as Kimberly watched out the window and Alex watched Kimberly. She was thinking deeply about something. The realization that he recognized Kimberly's thinking mode surprised him. They'd known each other for only four weeks, but he'd spent more time with her than most of the girl-friends he'd dated twice as long, and he'd rarely guessed their moods.

No one else was talking either, no doubt preoccupied with the envelope.

Back at the house, they gathered around the kitchen table. Elle set the bag containing the envelope in the center. Adam picked it up. "The postmark is San Francisco. Hardly helpful."

"May I see it?" asked Kimberly. "My name is written under the mailing label." She placed her thumbs to open the zip top.

"Don't open it." Andrew and Elle spoke at the same time.

Elle took the bag. "There is a chance there is some sort of poison in here. And we don't want to ruin any fingerprints, although your friend may have touched it several times."

"You mean like arsenic?" asked Kimberly.

"Possibly, or talcum powder as a scare tactic. That is why I put the plastic knife inside. With a bag this large, it shouldn't be too hard to use it as a letter opener. If that bag lives up to the adver-tisements, we should be safe if there is a dangerous substance inside." Elle lay the bag on the table and picked up the knife through the plastic.

"Brilliant! Where did you learn that?" asked Andrew.

"I've been studying everything I can get my hands on while sitting at the front desk. While this isn't exactly what they described on one of the security blogs, when I saw the two-gallon bags, I knew it was worth a try." Elle slipped the edge of the knife under the corner of the envelope.

"Just a moment." Alex turned to Kimberly. "Go watch from near the door. If anything happens, get out of the room first and ask questions later."

"But—"

"Great idea. Alex, I think you should join her. You too, Andrew. Get out of the house and call 911 and the agents if anything looks even a tiny bit off. I'd rather have the FBI laughing at us than something worse happen."

Alex herded them to the door to the garage, and Andrew held up the keys.

Elle slowly worked on the envelope.

"You know Alan will kill us if something happens to her," whispered Andrew.

"It was Elle's idea. We can't baby her because he wants us to." Alex kept a light grip on Kimberly's arm.

"Done. And no powder." Elle tipped the bag, and a birthday card slipped halfway out of the envelope.

"Can you get the card all the way out and open it?" asked Adam.

"I think so." Elle manipulated the bag for an eternal minute. "There. Definitely no powder."

Adam motioned the others over. "Let's keep it in the bag."

Kimberly's grip on Alex's hand tightened as they took their seats at the table. Her face lost all color. "That's Jeremy's handwriting."

"Are you sure?"

"Positive."

Kimberly traced Jeremy's signature through the bag. Seeing his handwriting on the envelope was more surprising than had there been anthrax in it.

"Can you read it?" Adam's question was loaded.

No, I might fall apart.

Kimberly turned the card so everyone could see.

February 12th

Dear Kimberly,

For the first time in six years, I am early. Which also means this probably won't be a very happy birthday as I am either missing or dead. I'm sending this to your friend since you are being watched. If you can, leave. I know you are expecting again, and I hope this time the baby stays where she should. Twelve weeks by my count. I know you think I don't know, but that is to protect you. The longer you can hide it, the better.

Look for flowers from the same florist I used the first time, to the same address, on your real birthday.

I hope this makes sense. I'm not good at the covert stuff.

I know I don't say it and I haven't really shown it. In fact, I've been a pretty awful husband. I hope to make it up to you and that you never see this card.

I love you. I am looking forward to Valentine's Day.

I hope you never have to read this. I hope I'm wrong.

Always,

Jeremy

PS. If Agent Miller is dead or missing, there is a mole in the FBI. Be careful.

He'd known about the baby.

Kimberly's heart thumped so loud she couldn't hear anything else. He'd known she was in danger. Why hadn't he warned her earlier? Maybe he thought he had time.

Alex's hand covered hers. No one asked any questions.

A JAR OF BATH BOMBS sat on the ledge next to one of the largest bathtubs Kimberly had ever seen, the water pouring from a waterfall faucet. Kimberly adjusted the temperature and looked for blinds or a curtain.

Upon further inspection, she realized that blinds were not required. The window faced the ocean, and the balcony didn't extend under the window. Still, Kimberly dimmed the light to barely brighter than a candle before getting undressed and stepping into the tub.

She chose a lavender bath bomb and chased it around the water with her hands as it sputtered and fizzed, soon disintegrating, leaving only the relaxing scent of lavender behind. The tub was perfectly situated to watch the stars flickering over the Pacific. Kimberly regretted not opening the window so she could hear the waves crash against the rocks below.

The baby kicked.

When Kimberly tried to push back, it rewarded her with two more kicks. She would never tire of this game. "So, little one, what did you think of Daddy's card?"

Kick.

"I don't know what to think either."

Nudge.

"He knew about you. I never would have guessed. You know, of all the things I've been upset with him about, his not knowing I was pregnant was the biggest worry. I never got to share you with him."

Push.

"But he knew. It isn't fair. I would have liked to have a memory of him holding us, just one night, just one hour. Instead, he moved to another bedroom. He said he wanted to protect us. But—" Tears streamed down Kimberly's face, and she slapped the water, splashing the window.

The baby didn't move.

"Are you listening?" Kimberly rubbed her stomach. "He tried to save us, but why didn't he tell me? Surely he could have found a way. And a birthday card? Why not something we could have found in March, like on St. Patrick's Day, or on Easter, in April? How dumb. We could have been killed!"

Kick.

"There you are. You don't like it when Mommy raises her voice? Sorry. I don't know what to feel. Sad, glad, mad, bad. I thought I had moved past what was once us. I thought I'd put things in perspective, but he knew about you. He knew we were in danger. Why didn't he save us before they killed him?"

Nudge.

"He couldn't have known. Maybe he thought he had longer. My birthday was almost a half year away. Who knows? The card doesn't give me enough information, and now I must go back to Indiana to get some flowers."

Roll.

"Oh, baby, what am I supposed to do? And feel?" I'll tell you one thing—you will never meet your slimeball of a grandfather." Jeremy said she was being watched. Did he know about the cameras? Kimberly watched a satellite cross the sky.

The camera in her studio had appeared two weeks after the funeral. Likely, the other ones had not been installed until then either. She hoped.

The moon looked down at her.

Kick.

"I don't know what to say. Can today be over? Or tomorrow? The funeral will not be pleasant. People will expect me to cry. I shed my tears for your grandma months ago. She would have liked to know you."

The first tears for her mother had come the day that, almost a year ago, her mother thought she was another nurse. Then the day Mom had said she didn't have a daughter. And then the day she had thought Kimberly was only sixteen.

She leaned against the tub. What was the point?

"Why? Why?" she asked the sky.

The stars guided the great explorers but gave her no direction.

"She is still in the bathroom." Elle sat down on the couch.

Alex tipped his chair back on two legs, trying to see up the stairs. "It's been over an hour. At what point should I worry?"

"Too late to ask. You are already worried." Andrew looked up from his laptop.

"What if she is stuck?" asked Alex

Adam set down the book he had been reading. "You could go talk to her the way you used to Abbie—through the door."

It was worth a try. Alex felt everyone's eyes on him as he ascended the stairs.

Kimberly's bedroom door stood open. He tapped on the bathroom door. Surprisingly, it was open a half inch.

"Kimberly?"

Alex waited, then tried again, louder.

"Alex? Don't come in."

"I won't. I wanted to make sure you're okay."

"I haven't drowned if that's what you mean."

Her answer was far from adequate. Her voice wasn't choked with tears—could she be in shock again? Not medically, although he had watched her for signs of shock after the ordeal with the police. "Do you want to talk?"

"I'm in the bathtub."

"I know. I'll stay out here. Abbie and I used to talk like this. I'd sit on the floor outside her bedroom or bathroom. My brothers would come and pretend to trip over my legs." Alex slid down the wall until he was sitting.

"Alex?"

"Yes?"

"What am I supposed to do?"

"About what?"

"Everything."

"That is a big question. Can you narrow it down?"

"I don't know. There is just so much. Too much. Mom, Jeremy, Hawthorn, baby, murderers, not trusting the FBI—and you. I don't even know where to start."

Me? That list was a heavy one to be included in. "What about your mother?"

"Tomorrow is her funeral, and I feel like I'm done mourning her. If I could, I would skip it, but everyone went to so much work to set it up. The church ladies are making us lunch after, although I told them there weren't any other family or friends than the five of us."

"Candace would have come."

"I know, but what if someone is watching me? I don't want anyone making the connection and putting her in danger too. Can you imagine? If someone realized I knew Candace, it could lead them to Mandy, Tessa, Candace's cousin, and their other roommate—what's-her-name."

"You mean Araceli?"

"That's her. I never met her. Anyway, if this is about money, I would be putting six billionaire families loosely tied to me in danger. That's why I told her not to come. It's a funeral."

Her logic was off. Even if someone tied the six families to her, the chances they would try going after the families were infinitesimally small. "I think this funeral is more about your California friends showing they love you."

Water splashed against the tub. "You're probably right. It was nice to get so many hugs tonight. That is one thing I've missed at the church in Chicago."

"Hugs?"

"No, friends. I don't really talk to anyone."

"Or I don't let you." Alex pulled his knees up.

"True, you can be a bit pushy."

"Just doing my job." He thought he heard a laugh. If only he were wittier.

"Thanks for not being pushy today."

"Mmm-hmm." His hours of conversation with Abbie had taught him that he could keep the conversation moving with any sound that proved he was listening.

"I think today may have been the hardest day of my life. The four of you are the only thing holding me together."

"I wish we could have spared you." The emotions he'd felt listening to Hawthorn over the FBI's wires that morning came back. He'd found himself wanting to hit a wall to work out the frustration. There had to be some exercise equipment in the house.

"Did I throw up on Agent Danes?"

"No, you missed him." *But I wish you hadn't.*

Splash. "Too bad. By the way, you handled my sickness well. Believe me, as much morning sickness as I've had over the years, I know when someone can—" She didn't speak for several seconds. "Sorry, I lost my train of thought." Kimberly spoke slowly, her voice deeper than before.

"It happens."

A few more splashes. "I think I have a problem."

Alex shot to his feet. "What?"

"There must have been oil in the bath bomb I used. The tub is really slick, and I don't dare stand up."

"Do you want me to get Elle?"

"I don't think she is tall enough to get me out of here. The tub is deep"

"But she can help."

"I'm so embarrassed."

Alex rubbed the back of his head. "Can you reach any towels from where you are sitting?"

Splash. Splash. "Yes, there are three of them."

"Good, let the water out. When it is empty, put one in the tub, like a bathmat."

He heard the water draining out of the tub. Faster than he expected, the sound deepened and slowed.

"It's empty."

"Can you stand up now?"

"I think so."

Alex listened for a thump or bump. He was ready to run in whether she was dressed or not. "Wrap up in the other towels. Don't try to get out. Your feet could be slippery.'"

"Okay."

"Are you decent?"

"As much as I can get. Fortunately, these towels are huge."

"Coming in." Alex pushed the door open; only the slightest glow came from the overhead lights, and the moonlight glistened off her shoulders. The way she held her arms around the towel reminded him of the *Birth of Venus* painting one of Candace's roommates had reproduced on a cupboard at Art House.

"This is so embarrassing."

"Better embarrassed than hurt." He held out his hand, but Kimberly shook her head.

"I'm afraid to let go of my towels. I don't think we are at a point where I can flash you without both of us dying of embarrassment."

True. "Do you trust me to scoop you out?"

Kimberly turned sideways. "Is this easier?"

Alex scooped her up and pulled her tight to his chest. *Now what?* The tile floor could be treacherous if she still had oil on her feet. He carried her to the bed and gently set her down, careful to not disturb the towels.

"Thanks, Alex." Her breath warmed his face.

Good thing there were no lights on. He was sure he was as red as the proverbial beet. Alex backed away. "Do you need anything?"

"Turn on the light as you leave?"

Alex crossed the room.

"And thank you."

"Anytime." He would have said, "As you wish," but she would probably understand too well what he was feeling. Everyone knew what those three little words really meant.

PASTOR BAXTER PROCLAIMED A BENEDICTION once the last notes of the organ had faded. Unlike Jeremy's funeral, there were no pallbearers and no dutiful following of the casket to a cemetery. Kimberly wasn't sure what to do. Quiet greetings filled the sanctuary as people filed out. Pastor Baxter came to stand in front of her and extended his hand. Kimberly shook it, Alex at her side. She glanced at the number of people between her and the door. More than hugs, she needed a bathroom, now. According to the maternity website, it was because her body was replacing amniotic fluid. It felt like the baby was using her bladder as a trampoline.

"Pastor, is there a secret passage to the restroom?" she whispered.

He smiled. "Not really, but if you use the side exit, you can go around the building."

Alex and Elle followed her dash for freedom.

Unfortunately, Agents Danes and Garcia did too. "Mrs. Thompson, please wait."

Kimberly sped up. Whatever they had to say could wait. She cut across the lawn, hurrying toward the next door.

Agent Danes ran to catch up, grabbing her arm. "Mrs. Thompson, we need to talk."

Kimberly shook her arm, but he didn't let go. "And I've been sitting in a pew for an hour, and I need to find the ladies room."

"This will only take a moment.'"

"So will going to the bathroom. Let me go." Kimberly used her free hand to loosen his grip.

"You heard her. Let her go." Alex glared down at the agent.

"Whose side are you on?"

"The pregnant lady's."

"Fine." Agent Danes dropped his hand. "Garcia, go with her."

Kimberly rushed into the building's rear entrance, closely followed by Agent Garcia and Elle. This felt like junior high, running into the bathroom with your two besties to get away from the boys so you could tell secrets. Only she had nothing to tell.

They had decided to not tell the FBI about the letter until they could talk to Deputy Assistant Director Hastings. The last thing they wanted to do was share their knowledge of a potential double agent with the wrong person.

Kimberly ignored her entourage and entered the bathroom, claiming the only empty stall.

Several women entered the restroom. She breathed a sigh of relief. The agents couldn't question her if she was talking to friends.

Gladys met her at the sink. "There you are. I told Maria you wouldn't have left and probably ran in here, being pregnant and all."

Kimberly washed her hands before Mrs. Scott enveloped her in a hug. "How are you doing, dear? That is quite the hunk you have with you. Do you young kids still use *hunk*?"

"I am well." Kimberly patted her stomach. "So is this one."

"And the guy?"

The mirror caught Kimberly's blush. "He is very fit."

Mrs. Scott laughed. "Glad you've kept your humor. If you don't want him, I'll take him. He is the perfect age."

Kimberly struggled to come up with a response to that.

"I'm always collecting extra grandsons—one never knows when one will need to move and can use the extra muscle." Mrs. Scott patted Kimberly on the arm and entered an empty stall.

Agent Garcia impatiently tapped her foot against the tile floor, as Mrs. Wallace started telling Kimberly about her newest grandchild and pulling out a slew of photos. Kimberly slipped out of the bathroom, Mrs. Wallace in tow. They walked to the fellowship hall, where only two small tables were set up for the funeral dinner. Eager to keep out of the agent's line of fire, Kimberly entered the kitchen and thanked each of the women there for preparing a meal, then gave them a hug. When she exited the kitchen, she directed the Hastings Security team to take their seats.

Pastor Baxter joined them. "Oh, do we not have enough plates?" He looked pointedly at the FBI agents.

"No, we're fine. Agents Danes and Garcia are looking for an opportune time to question me. Unfortunately, my mother's funeral dinner is not the time." Kimberly glared at the agents. Agent Garcia nodded and pulled Agent Danes from the room.

Dinner included baked ham, green-bean casserole, rolls, and a cheesy potato casserole Gladys referred to as funeral potatoes. Kimberly ate with the Hastings Security team. As the pastor spoke to Adam, Kimberly remembered the key he'd handed her last night. She opened her purse and dug around for it. Kimberly couldn't help but smile knowing her mother had saved it all these years. It was on the key chain she'd made at camp as a teenager. She leaned over to Alex. "We should probably go check on my mother's things."

Alex took the key from her. "We'll have to figure out a way to do it without being followed."

Kimberly was disappointed to find the church lobby still very much occupied after they finished the meal. Agents Garcia and Danes sat on the couch. It looked as if they had been arguing. They stopped talking when they saw her, and Agent Danes stood. "Mrs. Thompson, do you have time to answer a few questions now?"

Adam stepped forward. "Perhaps it would be better if we made an appointment to come speak with you. It may have escaped your notice that not only is this Mrs. Thompson's mother's funeral, she is quite fatigued."

Once again, Agent Garcia frowned at Agent Danes. She understood the inappropriateness of their actions. "Does this afternoon at three work for you?"

Kimberly consulted her phone. "Can we make it three thirty?"

Agent Garcia nodded and herded Agent Danes out the door.

Alex looked around before speaking. "We need to empty Kimberly's mother's storage unit. I would prefer to do it without the FBI following us."

"That may take a bit of planning. We had a tail this morning all the way to the funeral," said Andrew.

"I think I have an idea." Elle looked around nervously. "They know we only have one car, with tinted windows. It would be difficult to see inside. Assuming they are watching us now, we should all go back to the house. Then, at three o'clock, Andrew and Alex can go with Kimberly to the FBI office. Adam and I can go to the storage unit."

"One flaw with your plan—we only have one car," said Adam.

"What do you think Lyft is for? We get a ride to the nearest airport, then walk through and rent a second vehicle."

Andrew patted Elle on the shoulder. "Two more points for you for a good plan. The FBI is picking us up outside the gates to the community. Chances are that even if they're still watching, they won't be watching for whatever car comes to get you."

"I have one request. Can we return to Chicago tonight?" Kimberly fought to keep the fatigue out of her voice.

Alex put a supportive arm around her. "Whatever you need." Andrew led the way out of the building and into the waiting SUV. What she needed was a nap.

Alex sat down next to Kimberly and refastened his seat belt. "You sure you don't want to go back and lie down? We've reached cruising altitude."

Kimberly reached for his hand and laid her head against his shoulder. "I'd rather not be alone right now." She closed her eyes.

Alex reached over with his free hand and smoothed her hair. He didn't blame her. The interview at the FBI office had been frustratingly pointless. Most of the questions were a rehash of the questions she'd already answered. Fortunately, none of the questions pertained to the card Kimberly had received, and so she had not been forced to lie.

Kimberly rubbed his arm without opening her eyes as she spoke. "I'm going to move back to Art House tomorrow."

"Why so soon?"

"Preston's parents will come any day now, as will the triplets. Although no one will be crowded in the mansion, I assume the grandparents will want some quiet time away from three babies. Besides, it sounds like I need to be at Art House for the next clue."

"You should go lie down on the bed. You'll sleep better."

"I'm afraid of falling out of the bed if there's turbulence."

"We didn't have any coming out." Alex countered her argument.

"That doesn't mean we won't have any going back."

Alex thought for a moment, unsure how Kimberly would receive his next idea. "If you lie under the covers next to the wall and I lie on top of them, you should be secure."

Kimberly opened her eyes and turned her head to stare up at him, studying him for several long moments. Alex wondered if she could see more than his need to protect her. Could she see his need to hold her, or did he hide it well? Slowly, she nodded and pushed the button to bring her chair upright. Alex did the same.

By silent agreement, they left the sliding door to the bedroom open. Kimberly slipped off her shoes and put them in the drawer under the bed, as did Alex. He held up the blanket for Kimberly to climb under, then tucked her in before lying on the other side.

"What if you fall out?"

Alex settled his arm around her. "I guess I better hold on."

Kimberly snuggled into his embrace. "Good night, Alex."

"Good night, Kimberly."

Alex waited until Kimberly's breathing became even and deep, then he kissed the crown of her head and said the words he'd wanted to say all day. "I love you."

IT HADN'T BEEN THIS HARD to wait for a birthday since she was six. Not even the Independence Day celebrations had lessened the anticipation. Alex took several day trips to see his new nephews. Kimberly accompanied him twice, both times staying the night at his parents' as the six hours of travel was becoming more and more uncomfortable each week. At least it was a valid excuse to keep him at arm's length when she wanted to be held in his arms.

Elle's constant presence helped remind Kimberly that Alex was doing a job. Kimberly guessed Alex had had a conversation with Elle similar to the one she and Elle had the morning after they'd returned from California. The awkward conversation had boiled down to "Please protect Alex from me. Help me remember this marriage is fake. I don't want to ruin his life."

As the days fell into a routine, Kimberly spent a portion of each day in the studio. Alex worked remotely from his computer. And Elle read a lot. Kimberly caught only glimpses of the other two bodyguards as they stayed outside even when Alex went to Chicago. In the evenings, the three of them watched movies or television, Kimberly from the recliner, where she couldn't fall asleep on Alex's shoulder.

The only good news had been the FBI allowing her to have her June royalty check. Which she wouldn't see until the end of July, but it meant she could spend some of her stash without counting every penny, though the single check wouldn't go far toward paying Candace back or whatever the insurance-fraud fine would be.

Finally, her birthday arrived. To distract herself, Kimberly sketched different animals, trying to decide which one fit Mrs. Capps the best. So far, nurse owl was winning. What she wanted was to use the red cardinal who kept landing in the tree across the yard as a character, but it just didn't fit. Alex had removed the moratorium for keeping the blinds in the studio closed during the day and allowed her to walk around the fenced yard.

The doorbell rang, and her pen slipped, leaving a line across the owl's wing.

Kimberly checked the video feed on her phone, hoping this would be the delivery they were waiting for. It was the corner florist, the same one Jeremy had used when they were engaged. She waited for Elle to answer the door and accept the flowers before joining Alex and Elle in the kitchen.

The flowers themselves were unexceptional—in fact, they were rather patriotic. Mostly red, white, and blue—one of the hazards of a July birthday.

Alex handed Kimberly the card; the message was typed as if the flowers had been ordered over the phone or the internet.

Kimberly,

Happy birthday. I'm sorry to miss it this year. Sending a gift the day I normally get your present.
Love, Jeremy

PS. The key is for box 1932, in the town where I first told you I loved you.

She handed the note to Alex. "What key?"

Elle pulled a ribbon stamped "Key to my heart ... Key to my ... " from the arrangement. "This one?"

Alex took the key. "It looks like a standard PO box key. The question is where and when?"

"The thirty-first. Jeremy got my birth date mixed up when we first met. Every year he'd give me some little thing on my birthday, then, on the thirty-first, make a big production of the gift, claiming he forgot."

"I know that is personal, but where?" asked Elle.

"Shipshewana. He'd flown out to visit for the weekend, so I took him up to the Menno-Hof museum. Afterward, we were walking around, and there was a farmers' market. Most of the vendors were Amish. Jeremy was joking around and threatened to kiss me in front of them to see how many blushed, but I told him to stop, so he started yelling he loved me. I think I was the most embarrassed person there."

"Not something you would easily forget." Alex handed Kimberly the key.

"No." Had he been sincere, it would be a memory to cherish, not a way to leave a clue.

Elle scrolled through her phone. "There are two post offices there."

Alex checked his watch. "We could drive up today and check them out. I've had the Menno-Hof museum on my bucket list for a while. Then we can take you out for a birthday dinner."

"Have you been there, Elle?" asked Kimberly.

Elle shook her head. "I'd never even heard of it until I moved here."

"Let's go, then. I've been wanting to look at an Amish cradle. Since the FBI has unfrozen my June paycheck, I need to think of buying a few baby things. I have only six weeks left to prepare for this little one. Besides, this may be one of my last outings." Baby kicked Kimberly in the ribs in agreement. She winced and rubbed the spot.

"Another power kick?" asked Alex.

"I don't think your lecture last night worked." Kimberly rubbed the spot of the second kick. Every night since returning from California, they'd spent part of the evening reading or talking up in the loft. Her favorite spot was still in the beanbag chair, but with just over a month and a half left, getting out of it without help had become difficult.

"You sure you're up to it?" asked Alex.

"Half the museum is sitting and watching videos. I can do this." Kimberly led the way to Alex's truck. She wasn't going to miss a chance to go on an outing.

As suspected, the post-office box was empty except for several months' worth of generic circulars. At Kimberly's insistence, Alex added the key to his key ring. They arrived in time to join the next tour at the Menno-Hof. The rest of the tour group included a family with elementary-age children and grandparents. The grandfather kept pronouncing Amish as Aim-ish, causing his daughter to cringe.

After the tour, they drove a few blocks to the flea market. Alex expected a few stalls in a city park, not acres and acres of wares. Hand in hand, Alex and Kimberly wandered through buildings and stalls. Elle hung back, watching for trouble.

Kimberly stopped at furniture stalls and quilt stalls and clothing stalls. Elle seemed as enthralled with the wares as Kimberly did. And Alex found shopping at the flea market more fun than shopping on Fifth Avenue in New York. He kept a wary eye out for anyone paying more attention to them than to the conservative Mennonite and Amish families.

A rocking cradle suspended between two supports caught Kimberly's eye. She ran her hand over the smooth, dark wood as she spoke with the wife of the Amish crafter. Alex watched the conversation with only one eye as he'd noticed two over-dressed men following them. Someone had forgotten to tell the FBI agents they wouldn't blend in, in Northern Indiana dressed like city businessmen. Alex signaled to Elle to watch the men, then moved to Kimberly's side.

Kimberly bit her lower lip. "This one is my favorite so far. Part of me thinks I should stop looking. But I'm so not sure."

"Why aren't you sure?"

"I don't know. What if I'm wrong and the baby doesn't like it?"

The Amish woman hid a smile.

Alex turned Kimberly to him and raised her chin. "I might be wrong about this, but I think as long as the baby is loved, he or she won't care too much about the cradle—as long as there are no slivers. And this cradle is too finely made for any of those."

"You have a wise husband." The wife pulled a small mattress out of a box. "We will include this mattress for free."

Kimberly bit her lip again and nodded. "I'd like to buy it."

"How will you get it home?" asked the husband.

Alex measured the cradle with his hands. "I have a truck. It should fit in the back seat."

"It comes apart like this." The carpenter pulled two wooden pins out, unhooking the bassinet from the support stand. "Now it will fit?"

"Definitely."

"I'll wrap it for you. It will be about fifteen minutes, if you would like to look around."

"Thank you." Kimberly wandered out of the shelter of the stall.

Elle leaned against a post and nodded at the two men in suits. They stood out like oranges in a bushel of apples. "They've been looking at home decor."

Alex nodded. "Take Kimberly into the quilt booth. I will walk around to the horse auction. I want to see if they separate."

Elle and Kimberly crossed to another vendor, and Alex walked down the aisle toward the men, who turned their backs to him.

Amateurs. Alex entered the barn. Neither man followed him. Alex dialed his uncle only to get voicemail. He left a generic message, rounded the barn, and exited the other side.

Elle texted. **Both still following. Looking for a restroom.**

Alex found his way back to the furniture stall. The cradle was ready, and he couldn't see either of the men. The furniture maker carried the frame to the truck so Alex didn't have to make two trips. When it was loaded, he texted Elle. **Cradle in Truck. Leave or stay?**

—K wants to go home.

Come to truck. So much for a birthday dinner. Alex shifted to his backup plan. On the way home, they could stop at the Amish bakery and pick up Kimberly's favorite peanut-butter cookies, and brownies for Elle.

—Stopped at fudge stall.

Alex laughed. Maybe the bakery was out. A king-sized quilt hanging in the stall nearest him caught his eye, and he went to look at it while he waited for the women. The traditional design was in bold blues and greens, like one of the quilts Kimberly had admired in another stall. Alex checked the price. If they were not fake married, he wouldn't hesitate buying it as a birthday gift. But would she need a quilt that large? A small quilt folded on the corner of the table made of yellows and greens and edged with calico ducklings might be more appropriate, although it was more a gift for the baby. Alex rubbed the corner between his fingers. Soft, warm. Everything a baby could want, supposing he'd been right earlier. He handed the vendor some cash, and her daughter wrapped the quilt in brown paper.

—We are at the truck. Where are you?

Coming. Alex left the stall and jogged to the truck, passing the two men getting into a dark sedan.

As he approached his truck, he unlocked it with his key fob.

Elle climbed into the back seat next to the cradle. Alex handed her his package, then helped Kimberly up into the front seat.

"Why would the FBI be following me at a flea market?"

"I don't know. They were not at the museum or post office." Elle studied her phone.

"I tried to call Uncle Donovan, but he didn't answer. I am surprised the FBI is following you at all now that they released your funds." Alex turned onto the main road.

Elle leaned over the seat back. "They are so obvious. It's as if they got their training by mail order. And they were late to the party. No one followed us on our drive up here."

"We'd been in Shipshewana about two hours before they found us, right?" asked Alex.

"Closer to two and a half. They would have had time to drive from Chicago."

"Elle, when we get back, I want you to sweep everything. I want to figure out how they knew where to look for us today. I'm sure they haven't been watching the house."

"This was our first outing since California. Could that have triggered them? First we get a delivery, then we leave, and it is my birthday."

True, but that would mean they'd been watching and he hadn't noticed. Alex used the car system to call Alan. "Hey, we picked up two agents today. I'm worried they may have been monitoring us for a while and I missed it. Can you run a scan?"

"Sure, but I haven't seen anything irregular. Are they still following you?"

Alex checked his rearview mirror. "Like glue. I'd try to lose them, but they have to know we will end up back at Art House."

"Not necessarily. You may have done something to trip an alarm. Someplace you went where they expected you to go."

The mailbox. They wouldn't be able to get at the contents without a warrant, but they could watch it through the post office's security. "I think I know what tipped them off, which means they might not know about Art House."

"Then don't go there. Come back to the office, and we can play some parking-lot shell games."

"Will do. See you in about three hours."

Alex turned into the Walmart parking lot. "Let's make it look like we intended to go here. Kimberly, get a set of clothes and whatever else you need for two days and dump them in Elle's cart on the way to get some snacks. Elle—toothpaste, toothbrush, hairbrush for Kimberly. If these guys do what they did at the market, they won't pay attention to what Elle is buying."

"Walmart rarely carries maternity clothes. I don't know if they will have something I can wear."

"I'll buy whatever version of a tourist T-shirt I can find in the men's department. Considering the number of old shirts you've acquired from me, I should just loan you another one of mine."

Kimberly smiled. "Do you have any left?"

"Just a few. Let's go."

Kimberly squirmed in the front seat as they passed yet another green exit sign. She needed a bathroom and hoped they would get to the office soon. Alex's phone rang. He answered it on the car system. "Hello?"

"Change of plans. Come over to the house for dinner."

"Sure, Dad. Why?"

"Your mom's idea. Since this is Kimberly's birthday, a birthday dinner at our house makes it look like this was always your destination. I talked to my brother, and he wants to get a better look at the two following you."

"Not his?"

"Nope."

"Oh."

The tone of Alex's *oh* was enough to kick Kimberly's heart rate up a notch or two. Alex released one of his hands from the wheel and gave hers a reassuring squeeze. "See you at the house, then."

Kimberly waited for the call to disconnect before she spoke. "We can't go to your parents' house if those two aren't FBI. They may be—"

Elle laughed. "You underestimate Jethro Hastings's home. There isn't a cockroach that moves within two hundred yards of their house they don't know about. And there's the safe room. I'd been in the house at least a dozen times before Alan showed it to me, and I never guessed it was there. The house looks like any other upper-middle-class home on their street, but I bet it has more security than Abbie and Preston's."

Kimberly looked over her shoulder. "Really? It didn't seem like it had any security when I went there for dinner."

"Then we did it right." Alex turned off the freeway and looked in his rearview mirror. "And they are still with us."

A few turns later, he pulled into the driveway of his parents' home. As usual, he came around to help Kimberly out of her door. Over his shoulder, she noticed the men pulling off under the shade of a tree. "They are still here."

"I know. Ignore them." Alex lifted her to the ground.

They'd decorated the house with balloons, and a happy-birthday banner hung above the entrance to the dining room. Mrs. Hastings enveloped Kimberly in a hug. "Happy birthday! So glad you came. You remember where the bathroom is?"

Kimberly nodded, grateful Mrs. Hastings had recognized her most immediate need.

A few minutes later, Kimberly returned to a room full of familiar faces.

"We thought of shouting "Surprise!" But I told Adam that might not be the best thing to do when you have only six weeks left." September patted Adam's chest, and her daughter dove for him, yelling, "Da!"

"Abbie sends her regrets and asks you visit her in the morning." Mrs. Hastings handed Kimberly a glass of lemonade. "Andrew is putting the burgers on the grill. Dinner will be a few minutes.

Alex, show her the safe room. And I put her in Abbie's old room. There's a queen bed in there."

The momentary look of confusion on Alex's face caused Kimberly to wonder if there was anything unsaid in their conversation as she followed him down the hall past the bathroom to a linen closet. Alex opened the door and lifted one shelf. The closet rolled into the wall, revealing a room beyond. "You just lift on the shelf and the secret door opens. You can do it with one hand. September managed it while holding Harmony last February." Kimberly followed Alex into the room.

"Once you are inside, close this door. What you don't see is the linen closet moving back into place and the door shutting." Alex closed what looked like a vault door. "This room is soundproof, fireproof, and, well, pretty much everything but teenage-boy proof. Mom only survived a day and a half with the entire family on what was supposed to be a seventy-two-hour drill. Apparently the ventilation system didn't cope with teenage-boy sweat."

Kimberly couldn't help but laugh. Alex showed her around the rest of the room, including the monitors to the outside. "If anything happens, get in here as fast as you can. Even if Elle, my mother, and I don't make it, if we yell at you to close the door, lock yourself in."

"Will it come to that?"

Alex looped an arm around her shoulder. "I hope not, but we are Hastings. I think preparing for the worst and hoping for the best is in our blood."

He turned on the outside monitor. Down the street, the car still sat with both men inside.

"Elle wasn't exaggerating when she said nothing goes unnoticed here, was she?"

"Only a little. We don't know anything that goes on in our neighbors' houses. But this is the wrong street to steal a package off someone's porch."

"I pity the person who tries to get one off of your parents' porch."

"He'd get dropped into the dungeon, like in the old black-and-white movies."

"Really?"

Alex laughed. "No, although we designed one to do that when we were teens. This house doesn't have a basement. We wanted to try it on Abbie's mansion, but Preston said no."

"I'm almost disappointed."

"Come on, let's go celebrate your birthday."

26

"WHAT ARE YOU DOING DOWN here?" Mom said as she entered the family room.

Alex pointed at the monitors. "Watching our unidentified watchers."

"Andrew can do that. You need to be upstairs with your wife."

"Mom, we're not—"

Mom held up a hand. "I've watched you throughout dinner. Have you told her yet?"

"Told her what?"

"That you love her."

"Not when she's awake."

Mom crossed her arms and rolled her eyes. "Your *wife* is upstairs pacing the floor. Go to her and tell her the truth. And don't use some excuse about grayed lines. Love doesn't care if she's a client or not."

Alex's jaw dropped as he searched for an answer.

"Don't make me count, Alex. I'm still your mother. I will."

Still, Alex stood rooted to the spot.

"Ten, nine, eight—"

As if he were still a ten-year-old, Alex's body responded, fearing what would happen if Mom ever reached one.

The lamp in Kimberly's room glowed from beneath the door. "Kimberly?"

The door opened, and Kimberly stepped back, letting him in. "Can't you sleep?"

"Not with the little one playing hopscotch." The fatigue in her eyes told of other reasons.

"May I?" Alex's hand hovered over her belly.

Kimberly nodded.

Alex knelt so his face was level with the baby and placed his hands on either side of Kimberly's stomach. "Hey, little one. It's time to go to sleep now. You are keeping Mama up, and she's had a hard day. It was her birthday, and plans didn't work out so well."

Kick.

"He doesn't want to listen to you either."

Alex met Kimberly's eyes. "So it's a boy?"

"I think it's an entire rugby team."

Kick.

"That will not make more room in there. I could sing, but it would probably hurt your mama's ears."

Kick.

"Oh." Kimberly rubbed where her ribs met the bulge.

"That's not a very nice way to treat the woman I love."

"What?"

"I said he shouldn't—"

Kimberly put her hand on Alex's cheek. "Do you really?"

Alex covered Kimberly's hand, keeping it in place as he stood. "Yes. I've been saying it for weeks now, but only when you are sleeping."

"I thought I was dreaming. I think I heard you."

"I know it is probably too soon—"

Kimberly covered his mouth with her own before he could say anything stupid. Alex buried one hand in her hair, pulling her close. The kiss was worth the wait. Alex slid his arm around her waist and deepened the kiss.

Kick.

Kimberly pulled back and laughed. "Now he got you in the stomach."

"You're sure she isn't a girl? A boy wouldn't have interrupted our kiss."

"Stay with me tonight?" A blush bloomed in her cheeks.

"Really?"

Kimberly nodded. "Just to sleep. We can't—"

"But we can kiss." Alex bent his head and pulled his wife into another kiss, ignoring the protests of the baby, who kicked him soundly in the gut.

Kimberly slipped out of bed and into the bathroom. If baby wasn't kicking her ribs, he was bouncing on her bladder. As she exited the en-suite bathroom, she took a moment to study her husband in the early morning light creeping through the window. At some point he'd changed into a pair of pajama pants, his shirt gone. Kimberly covered her mouth. If she'd seen him with his shirt off earlier… but that wasn't love. He'd said he loved her. Kimberly tried to find the words to say it back, but the lie she had uttered so many times with Jeremy wouldn't come.

Did she love him or need him?

Whatever chemicals his kisses had released in her brain had soothed her more than any box of chocolates. Waking to find him protectively curled around her made her feel safer than the secret room downstairs ever could. But was that love?

Rather than climb back in bed and lose herself in his arms, Kimberly gathered her things to take a shower.

And locked the door.

Andrew paced the family room. They'd postponed the visit to Abbie's because of the suits still watching the house. Uncle Donovan had confirmed the men were not employed by the bureau, but since they hadn't done anything illegal yet, there wasn't much they could do except wait.

Adam tapped on his tablet. "We can play musical cars with them."

"What if they follow the right car?" asked Kimberly from the recliner.

"We make them follow the wrong car. The only problem is finding doubles for you and Alex."

Elle looked up from her latest book. "You only need one good one. From a distance, both Adam and Alan pass as Alex. I'm close enough to Kimberly's height that with a wig and a small pillow, I could be a decoy."

Predictably, Alan frowned, but everyone ignored him.

"From a distance, I can pass as Kimberly too, but up close, my wrinkles would ruin it." Mom patted her cheeks.

Dad leaned over and kissed Mom. "What wrinkles?"

"The ones you need to put on your readers to see." Mom kissed him back. "So we have two decoys."

"Where to do this, then?" asked Alex.

"The mall," Dad said. "Saturday is always crowded. Melanie, break out your costume kit and see what we can do about duplicating Kimberly. We leave here in three different cars. Elle goes to the mall with Adam and Kimberly in the truck, Melanie and Alex in Adam's SUV, and Alan in his car alone. Andrew and I will monitor things. We need to see if we flush out more tails." Dad handed out the assignments. "At the mall, you'll go to a changing room. Elle and Melanie will be transformed into Kimberly, who will be transformed into a different woman. Then you'll play musical cars and fake brothers. Alex, when it's clear, you leave in Adam's SUV with Kimberly and head to C&O's hangar, and we fly you two back to Indiana. I'll dispatch another team there with your truck as soon as I can. My guess is they don't know where you came from, only that you arrived in Shipshewana, and that limits our safe-house options. Kimberly, you are doing a home birth, correct?"

"Yes, the doctor cleared me for it right after we returned from California."

"Good. That will keep you out of any computer databases." Dad took notes on his tablet.

Mom came back in with Elle. The wigs and clothing were close enough. Mom also carried three identical Cubs baseball caps and sets of sunglasses. "Yay for sunny July days. Now, boys, shirts are a problem. I don't know that we have three matching shirts in the house."

Adam raised a hand. "I have a package of gray T-shirts in my car."

"Perfect. Only Alex leaves in the gray shirt." Dad pulled up the mall map and marked the various parking areas. Mom pulled Kimberly aside and showed her how to put on the blonde wig, then gave her a different shirt to wear. All the women put their costumes in various department-store shopping bags.

Mom and Alex left first. The men in the car didn't follow them.

Adam left with Kimberly and Elle, the tail on them before they exited the subdivision.

As planned, they met in the second-floor restrooms. Alex waited for the texts indicating that the two groups of impersonators had left before meeting Kimberly in a children's clothing store around the corner from the bathrooms. At first he didn't recognize her in her baby-pink blouse and blonde wig. They made a purchase and left through the mall's parking garage in Adam's SUV.

Forty minutes later, they were in the small jet owned by C&O and flying back to Indiana. Kimberly leaned back in her seat and breathed deeply.

"Is everything all right?"

"I don't know. I think it's stress. And Braxton Hicks contractions. I probably shouldn't be flying."

"As soon as we land, I'll call Mrs. Capps."

Kimberly clutched his hand. "Can you also call for a few quiet days?"

"I'll do that." Alex put his arms around her and held her close.

MRS. CAPPS FINISHED HER EXAMINATION. "Everything looks good. There are no contractions now, and nothing indicates actual labor. However, you need to stop gallivanting all over the place for a few days. Watch some movies. Read a few books. If you were Amish, I'd tell you to knit, but only in a reclining position."

Kimberly sat up. "What about painting?"

"All hunched over your easel? No. In the recliner in the front room, yes." Mrs. Capps put her stethoscope back in her bag. "I will tell Alex to pamper you as much as possible."

"He already does."

Mrs. Capps pulled a piece of paper from her bag. "There is a birthing class this Tuesday and Thursday night at the community center. You two need to come. If you can't make it, there is a way you can see it online."

Kimberly followed Mrs. Capps out to the living room, where the midwife repeated the instructions to Alex.

Alex closed the door behind her. "Anything I can do for you at the moment?" The softness in his eyes reminded her of his words last night.

"No, I'm going to take a nap." At his nod, Kimberly waddled as fast as she could to her room. For the first time since California, they were alone in the house.

Kimberly lay down with her tumultuous thoughts. Was letting Alex into her life the right thing to do?

Alex set his phone down. It had only taken the men who'd tailed them a day to give up watching his parents' house. Sunday afternoon, they'd simply started the car and driven off. Two days later, the car had turned up abandoned in a grocery-store parking lot.

Hastings assigned two new bodyguards to Indiana, but both were to watch from a distance. The less traffic around Art House, the better.

It was quiet. Too quiet. Other than to discuss the baby or what to eat, Kimberly hadn't spoken for two days. Alex went to search for her and, predictably, found her in the loft.

She was crying.

"What's wrong?"

Kimberly shook her head. "Everything. Nothing. Not the baby."

"Do you want to talk?" Alex sat in the beanbag next to hers.

"Want to know something funny?"

"Sure."

"Everyone thinks I named this Lover's Loft because I made out with so many guys up here. I didn't. Not once. I had a couple of first kisses and slapped one guy, but I never—well, not like Candace thought. It was the stars. I named it for the stars."

Alex settled into his beanbag and rolled onto his side. "Is there a constellation or something?"

"Not that I know of. I'd seen some movie about lovers remembering each other in the stars, and it just sounded right."

Alex leaned close enough to kiss Kimberly if she turned her head his direction. "We could solve the making-out part."

Kimberly put her hand on his chest and pushed him away.

"No, we can't. I wish we could. I really do. I want to cuddle with you every night, but it wouldn't be fair to you. I lied to Jeremy for years when I told him I loved him. I can't do that to you. I wish I could, but you bring out the part of me that needs to be as honest and decent as you are. I need your protection. I want the love you give me, but as deeply as I have searched my heart, I don't feel what I need to. Maybe I'm broken. Maybe it's pregnancy. I don't know." Kimberly took a deep breath as tears wound their way down her cheeks. "But it isn't fair to keep using you for my comfort."

Was she trying to break up with him? "Swee—Kimberly, I don't feel used, and I know this has got to be the most emotionally confusing time in the world for you. I'm willing to wait it out. If me holding you brings you comfort or peace, why stop?"

"Because I don't want to hurt you. I don't want you to believe in a lie that is not me. I don't want you to love me if I can't love you back."

Too late. Alex found her hand. "I'm a big boy. Let me worry about my heart. If I'm willing to love you and hold you knowing you might leave, that is my problem, not yours."

"I do sleep better when you are near. That's the part where I feel I am using you the most."

Alex reached out and wiped away a tear. "Thank you for being honest. What do you want to do now?"

"Look at the stars."

Alex rolled onto his back and wished for a falling star.

KIMBERLY MARKED ANOTHER DAY OFF the calendar. Thirty-seven weeks. Mrs. Capps would be over later today, and in four days, they could go open the PO box. With any luck, they would solve everything before the baby came.

Except for what to do about Alex.

Her honesty wasn't working out so well. He was more attentive than ever, and she was more confused. Kimberly escaped to the loft with a book. Perhaps getting lost in someone else's imagination would help.

Elle came up the stairs. "Mrs. Capps called. She needs to reschedule because her daughter is sick and someone is in labor."

Kimberly rolled over in the beanbag and used her index finger as a bookmark. "How do people know they're in love?"

Elle sat in the other beanbag. "I don't know. I don't think it's like the books. Take the one you are reading. Halfway through, Mr. Darcy declares his love, but is that what it is? Maybe. He has seen Elizabeth's wit and some of her kindness, and I don't think it's lust, although who knows? Miss Austen would not mention more than her fine eyes. Half the romance novels out there are talking about lust. How fast can people steam up the pages? I think at the time of the second proposal, Elizabeth truly admired Mr. Darcy, but did she love him, or did she love Pemberley? What if we could see them ten or fifty years later? I think love is something that takes time to grow. There must be a certain level of attraction first, but if the feelings don't continue to grow..." Elle shrugged. "But what do I know? I have a crush on a guy who doesn't even know I exist."

"I don't think Alan ignores you as much as he worries about the hero-complex thing."

"Abbie warned me about crushes on my bodyguard, but it has been months. I think if Alan were just a crush, it would have been over by now. I've seen him where he wasn't at his best enough to know the real Alan."

Kimberly pushed herself up. "Wait, what? Alan was your body-guard?"

"For two weeks. You didn't know?"

Kimberly shook her head. "No, but that explains a lot. Like why he is overprotective of you."

Elle rolled her eyes. "Ya think? But my story isn't the one that matters right now. I'm assuming we are talking about you and the bodyguard you married, which is complicated because you are carrying your dead husband's child and are technically paying your current husband to be your bodyguard or your bodyguard to be your husband, depending on which role comes first in your life."

"That was supposed to sound less complicated when you said it."

Elle shrugged. "Life is complicated. People who say it isn't are in denial or delusional. There will not be a less complicated time to work things out. But that isn't saying you have to work every-thing out today. Look at Adam and September. She knows she will marry him. We know she will marry him. But she's giving herself a year to make sure she is marrying him for the right reasons. Give yourself time. You don't need to run out and get a divorce the moment the baby is born or your husband's killer is found. The two of you have been in a highly stressful situation. If you weren't married, Jethro would probably reassign Alex."

"But he loves me so much more—" Kimberly covered her mouth, embarrassed.

"Mr. Darcy loved Elizabeth first. Does first mean more?"

Kimberly didn't have an answer for her.

Alex heard a cupboard in the kitchen close, then the refrigerator open. He picked up his phone to check the time, the screen illuminating the room. 1:47 a.m., July 31. Out of habit, he slipped on his shoes before going to the kitchen.

Kimberly stood in front of the refrigerator, a finger on her chin.

"Can't sleep?"

She closed the fridge. "No, and nothing sounds good. Nothing feels good." She tried to reach around her back.

"Would you like another back rub?" One of the massage techniques he'd learned at the prenatal class seemed to help her aching back.

"Do you mind?"

"Not at all. I'll get the tennis ball and meet you in your room." Alex checked the security cameras. Nothing. Good. One of the guys over at the caretaker's house was logged in and monitoring things. Alex signed off without checking in. The pattern had been the same for the past several nights. He'd get up in the middle of the night, check in, and coax Kimberly back to sleep. Sometimes twice. If she would stop being so stubborn and let him sleep with her when they went to bed in the first place, they would both get more sleep.

Kimberly sat on the side of her bed with the lamp on. "Sorry I woke you."

Alex sat behind her and placed his thumbs on either side of her spine. "Really? I thought you would be glad you woke me." He kneaded his way up to her midback and back down.

"Mostly sorry?" Kimberly leaned into his touch.

215

"I'll accept that. Is it only the baby keeping you up?"

"No, today is the day there should be something in the mailbox. I've thought up so many scenarios for what could be in there. I can't wait to open it, but at the same time, I hope it's empty."

Alex used the tennis ball to massage her lower back. "I don't think you should come."

"I know. Mrs. Capps doesn't want me to go either. She says I'm more dilated than she expected. But I still want to go."

"I'll bring you back some of those peanut butter cookies you like so much."

"What if I have to sign something?"

"I can take Elle. She has the wig and can wear one of your maternity tops. I think Mom even sent her down with some colored contacts. It should be good enough."

"This is one of those times you will not give me a choice, isn't it?"

"Do you think I should?"

Kimberly stretched her neck. "No. If those guys are waiting for us to show up at the post office, I can't run."

Alex didn't comment. Kimberly's waddle wasn't fast enough to beat a turtle. "Do you need me to rub your feet too?"

"No."

Kimberly lay down on her left side. Alex continued to rub her back, neither of them talking.

After a few moments, her breathing slowed. Alex laid down next to her, determined at least one of them would sleep.

Kimberly dried off from her shower as best she could. Having a real husband would be helpful right now as reaching her calves was nearly impossible. There was a sudden strong contraction—stronger than usual. Kimberly rested her hand on her middle until it subsided.

Labor?

Maybe.

Kimberly dressed and towel dried her hair.

Another significant contraction tightened her belly. She looked at the time on her phone.

Eight minutes later, while pouring a glass of milk, she felt another one.

Elle came into the kitchen in Kimberly's second favorite maternity top. With the brunette wig and brown contacts, Elle might pass a quick ID check, but nothing could be done to make Elle two inches shorter or change the shape of her face. Elle spun in a circle. "What do you think?"

Kimberly lowered herself into a chair. "I think you are way to agile for a woman in your condition."

"So a jump flip is out of the question?"

A laugh bubbled up. Kimberly attempted to suppress it knowing it would cause problems, but it was no use. "Please stop. Laughing makes me need to run to the bathroom."

Alex entered the kitchen. "Sam and Dave should be here in about fifteen minutes. They will keep watch from outside. If anyone other than Mrs. Capps comes to the door, they will take care of it." Alex's phone rang. He left the room to take it.

Elle sat at the table, frowning at her phone.

"Is something wrong?"

Elle typed into her phone, thumbs flying. "Not sure."

Alex came back into the room. "We need a new plan. Dave has food poisoning or something."

"Alan texted the same thing. He also thinks going to the post office first thing in the morning is a mistake if they're watching. He suggests waiting about an hour after the main office has closed." Elle managed to talk and text at the same time.

"Why not now?" Her contractions were between eight to twelve minutes apart, but that could change in eight or nine hours.

"What's Alan's reasoning?" asked Alex.

Elle looked up from her phone. "The PO boxes are still accessible when the office is closed, so any employees will have left. Also, it isn't as likely that there will be other people around if things get dangerous."

"Makes sense. That also gives Dave time to recover or me to find a local security guard to fill in for him."

"Ugh, I hate waiting." The weak argument wouldn't sway them. Hiding her phone under the table, Kimberly googled ways to stop contractions. Drinking water and lying on her left side. Both were doable and wouldn't seem out of the ordinary. "Anyone want to join me for a *Poldark* marathon?" *Please say no.*

"I think I'll pass. I'll go over to the caretaker's house and see how sick Dave is." Alex left the kitchen with a wave.

"I'm on duty. No *Poldark* for me." Elle started texting again.

Kimberly filled the large water bottle and returned to her room. She drank as much as she could before lying down. "Okay, baby, today is not a good day. Can you wait until tomorrow?"

ALEX EYED THE CLOUDS GATHERING in the western sky as he drove north. "Elle, what does your phone say the weather is?"

Elle consulted her phone. "Looks like we are in for a thunderstorm. According to the NOAA, it is only a severe-storm watch, not a warning."

"I hope something goes according to plan soon."

"Some plans come together in ways we don't expect. Rain at the post office will make it easy to see if someone is waiting for us. No one sits around in the rain."

"True." Alex took the turnoff to Shipshewana. "I'm more worried about the transformer down near Art House. It seems to go out every time lightning strikes within a hundred-mile radius."

"It hasn't gone out since the night Kimberly broke into the house. Stop worrying about her. She has Mrs. Capps next door, and Dave is feeling much better."

Stopping worrying? Was that even possible? Something had been off with Kimberly all day. And it wasn't the normal internal war she played with herself about her feelings for him. Maybe it was the worry about the contents of the mailbox. They'd all been on edge for days.

The phone rang. The console screen read "Jethro Hastings."

"Hey, Dad."

"Who's with you?"

"Elle. We are about ten miles from the post office."

"Sam and Dave are with Kimberly?"

"Just outside the house. Why?"

"Your uncle called. There was an attack on Agents Danes and Garcia. Garcia is in critical condition, and Danes is missing."

"When did this happen?" The first drops of rain splattered the windshield.

"Last night. They left Garcia for dead. I don't like the timing."

"Did Uncle Donovan ever tell anyone about the treasure hunt Jeremy is leading Kimberly on?"

"No point yet, but the timing of this attack—I don't like it."

"We'll be careful." Alex glanced at Elle.

"Be more than careful."

"Will do."

"Call me when you finish." The call disconnected.

The rain fell harder.

Elle straightened her wig. "I think I should go in. The building is a brick stand-alone, and the surrounding buildings should be closed. We can get one of those rain ponchos at the dollar store. It will be impossible to tell I am not Kimberly unless a person gets close enough I can flip them."

Alex considered Elle's plan. "You know Alan will kill me if anything goes wrong."

"Only after he locks me away like Rapunzel."

Alex pulled into a dollar-store parking lot. "Stay here. If someone is already watching us, your waddle isn't very convincing."

"I'll take that as a compliment."

Alex dashed into the store as the first clap of thunder sounded.

Kimberly stood in a puddle in the middle of the kitchen. It wasn't as big as she expected from the movies. She grabbed a wad of takeout napkins and dropped them onto the puddle, then used her foot to mop it up. It was time to make the call. Kimberly scrolled to Mrs. Capps's number.

"Hi. It's Kimberly. My water broke."

Alex watched Elle waddle into the post office from the parking lot of the law office across the street. They'd set her phone to record, and Alex watched his phone as she entered the empty lobby and opened the mailbox. A thick manila envelope lay inside. Elle pulled it out. "It's the only thing in here." Her quiet announcement sounded in his earpiece.

A door creaked.

"Mrs. Thompson, hand over the envelope."

Alex didn't wait to see what happened next but sprang out of his truck. He could still hear the sounds through his earpiece.

"No!"

Ooooomph!

Crash

Thump.

Alex entered the post office and found a man facedown on the floor, Elle's knee against his back. She pointed at the door to the supposedly closed service area. "I didn't see anyone else."

Alex ran to the door. Only the security light shone. No one else seemed to be around. He returned to Elle and the man struggling to free himself. "Where is your partner?"

"Where is yours?"

Elle bent the man's arm behind him. "Mr. Alexander asked you a question."

The man laughed. "He knew you wouldn't bring the real Mrs. Thompson out here—too risky."

Alex lifted the man's head by his hair. "Where is your partner?"

"With yours."

Crap!

"Dial 911!" commanded Elle.

"What is your emergency?" a woman's voice came over Elle's speakerphone.

"I was attacked in the Main Street post office!"

"Are you still there, ma'am?"

"Yes." Abbie's self-defense class had paid off. "I'm sitting on him now." Elle waved at Alex and mouthed, "Go!"

Alex ran for his truck, wishing it had wings.

"How long have you been having contractions?" Mrs. Capps eyed Kimberly suspiciously.

"They were about eight minutes apart this morning, but they stopped for a...while." Kimberly breathed through another one while Mrs. Capps finished her examination.

"I suspect this one will be born before the night is over. Where is Alex?"

"He and Elle ran an errand."

"I noticed those two guys sitting out in front of the house. Are they here for you?"

"Yup." Kimberly kept her answer short, waiting for the pain to dissipate.

Outside, the thunder clapped.

"I should have known. Babies enjoy coming during storms. Let's walk around while you still feel like it. I won't do a water birth during thunderstorms. Lightning can travel through the pipes, and even though the pool we'll use isn't connected to the house, I have to get the water from somewhere."

Kimberly nodded. "I understand." In the past few days, she'd nixed a water birth anyway because she wasn't prepared to have

Alex see that much of her, and chances were good that she might need his help to support her.

Kimberly began a slow circuit of the hallways, Mrs. Capps at her side. She turned at the library, but Mrs. Capps continued straight.

"Stop! It's a wall!"

Mrs. Capps put up her hand in time. "Well, I never. It's so real. Who painted an imaginary hall? Were they trying to kill someone?"

When Kimberly paused to breathe through the next contraction, Mrs. Capps rubbed her back. The lights flickered.

"Oh no. Not tonight!" Mrs. Capps yelled at the overhead light. It flickered again and went out.

The small lights above the main doors came on.

"What are those?"

"Emergency lighting—part of the alarm system. There are several battery-powered lanterns too."

Someone pounded on the front door.

"That must be the bodyguards."

Mrs. Capps went to answer it, Kimberly waddling after her.

"Where is she?" The voice was angry.

"Get out!" Mrs. Capps yelled.

A slap and a thump were followed by a cry from Mrs. Capps. Kimberly stood rooted to the spot as another contraction seized her.

"Mrs. Thompson? Or should I say Mrs. Hastings? Where are you?" The man's footsteps went up the other hall. The problem was, the hallway was one big circle. Kimberly moved as fast as she could to the front of the house, reaching for her cell phone, only to realize it was back in her bedroom.

Mrs. Capps lay on the living room floor, clutching her side.

Kimberly needed her phone. Or did she? Alex said the house had ears.

"Penguins! Penguins!"

"There you are." Agent Danes was pointing a gun at her.

Kimberly screamed and prayed that, despite the outage, whoever was monitoring the house had heard her.

ALEX DROVE AS FAST AS he dared in the pouring rain, praying all Amish buggies were safely off the road.

The car phone system beeped four times. Kimberly had activated an alarm. The audio came through the speakers.

"Agent Danes, what are you doing here?"

"You have information I need."

"No, I"—Kimberly gasped for breath as her abdomen tightened yet again— "don't."

"Oh, have I come at a bad time? Where is your normal bodyguard anyway? This old lady isn't one. She's dressed Amish. And the two in front of the house won't be in for a while."

"She's my midwife."

"Oh, and you are in labor." The agent's voice sounded sickly sweet.

Alex hit the button on the dash, calling the office. "Are you getting this? Where are Sam and Dave?"

Alan's voice came over the line. "They aren't responding. Their phone locators are putting them outside the house."

"Have you called the police?"

"Along with everyone else. There are power lines down everywhere. I'll keep trying."

Alex listened to the audio.

"Don't touch me." Kimberly's voice was strong.

"I have a man waiting at each of the post offices in Shipshewana. Whatever your first husband sent, we will get it, and you will be a widow twice in less than a year."

"You lie—" Kimberly doubled over.

"Oh, another contraction in less than two minutes? I think I have a better idea."

"What?" Kimberly's voice sounded strangled.

"Let's wait for nature to take its course. When the baby is here, you won't be strong enough to stop me, and I'll trade the baby's life for the information you won't give me now."

Kimberly's next words sounded like the same profanities going through Alex's head.

Alan's voice interrupted the feed. "I show you are five minutes away. The police said they can have a car there in fifteen. If someone is armed, they won't send in an ambulance until the place is cleared. Uncle Donovan is sending the nearest agents, ETA thirty minutes."

"Do you have any video?"

"No video. The house is on backup electricity, and Kimberly's phone is in her room. But the front-room audio is picking up the strongest."

"Can you open the studio door?"

"Studio door and garage side door are both unlocked."

Alex turned onto the street behind Art House.

"I'm here."

Kimberly leaned over the back of the recliner. Contractions at gunpoint. Too bad she didn't have a birth photographer. She'd be a social media hit. She winced at the crazy thought.

Mrs. Capps's pale face reflected pain as bad, if not worse, than

Kimberly's. The bonnet Mrs. Capps always wore lay askew, the midwife's gray hair spilling around her head on the floor. The lack of blood on the green dress was of little comfort. Mrs. Capps met Kimberly's eyes and breathed with her, coaching her through the next contraction. As soon as it cleared, Kimberly replied, "Agent Danes, you've been asking me for information for months now. You've searched my home. I don't have any!"

"Not yet. It should arrive today. Your husband was too smart for us. He made a backup plan. Why do you think we had to wrap his car around a tree? Two hours and all we got off him was your name and "ship she's on a." Not until you showed up in Chicago did we stop looking for cruise ships, fishing boats, or any ship you could be on. Who knew Shipshewana was a place? That's why Hastings went to the post office, isn't it?"

"He went to pick up a—" Focusing on Mrs. Capps, Kimberly panted through the next contraction.

"What did you say?"

Mrs. Capps raised her head. "Can't you see she is in the last stages of labor? Stop badgering her with questions."

Kimberly rested her head against the back of the recliner.

Mrs. Capps glared at the agent. "Make yourself useful. Put up the gun and get a stack of towels from the bathroom."

Agent Danes looked from one woman to the other. "I guess neither of you is going anywhere." He holstered his gun. "Where's the bathroom?"

Kimberly waved at the hall. "First door on left."

"You are doing well. Keep breathing. Do you feel like you need to push yet?" asked Mrs. Capps.

Kimberly shook her head and started breathing through the next contraction.

Thump! Thump!

Kimberly tried to turn her head toward a commotion coming from the bathroom, but the contraction held her in place. She'd lied. Pushing felt like a good idea.

A smile crossed Mrs. Capps's face as she continued breathing with Kimberly. "Good. Blow out now."

Kimberly pursed her lips.

"Thank you."

Startled by Alex's deep voice, Kimberly screamed. Mrs. Capps grimaced.

Kimberly clutched the back of the recliner and cried out.

"It's okay. You're safe."

Kimberly groaned.

"Alex, wash your hands and get the stack of sheets and towels from Kimberly's room now!"

Alex rushed to fulfill Mrs. Capps's commands.

He returned to find the midwife using a more soothing voice. "It will be all right. All he will do is catch the baby. I can't get up."

"Call 911."

Mrs. Capps winced. "They won't be here in time."

"How ... do ... you ... know ... ?" Kimberly panted between each breath.

Mrs. Capps pointed. "Kimberly, stay where you are. You can deliver standing or squatting. Gravity will help, and so will Alex."

"I can't—" Alex needed someone who had experience.

"Can and will. Kimberly is doing all the work. You just support your wife's weight."

Kimberly moaned.

"Kimberly, I need Alex to tell me if he sees the head. Alex, don't be a prude." Mrs. Capps voice grew fainter with each sentence.

To his surprise, Kimberly pulled up her nightshirt. "I don't care, Alex. Just get it out!"

"I see the head!"

"Do you see anything resembling a cord?"

"No."

"Good." Mrs. Capps pushed herself up on one elbow. "Kimberly, if you feel like pushing with this next contraction, push."

Kimberly grabbed Alex's hand, her nails biting into his skin as she bore down, but Alex forgot about his own pain when the head appeared.

"Good job. Breathe, and the next contraction will be your last... okay, push! You're doing great."

Alex put one hand under the baby's head, the other under its back.

"It's a boy." Alex stated the most obvious.

"Wrap him in one of those blankets. Cord can wait. Kimberly, sit up if...you..." Mrs. Capps's voice faded.

"Mrs. Capps!"

Alex looked over at the unconscious midwife, then back at Kimberly.

"Go." She nodded toward Mrs. Capps. Alex turned the recliner around so Kimberly could sit down with the baby.

A voice in his ear reminded him Alan was still listening. "Paramedics one minute out. Police and FBI in three."

Alex checked Mrs. Capps's pulse. "I think she fainted."

He could hear the sirens blaring.

"Give me a blanket! I don't want to be so exposed."

Alex hurried to comply as red-and-blue flashing lights lit the room.

Kimberly held her baby tight as a flurry of activity erupted around them, the medical personnel and police calling out to each other across the room and throughout the house. After being in the low-wattage emergency lighting for so long, the high-powered flashlights were blinding. Her baby cried, and the shouting stopped.

Alex knelt by her side as he spoke to the EMTs. "See to Mrs. Capps first. I think he threw her against the wall. She said she couldn't get up. I tied the perp up in the bathroom. He will tell you he's FBI, which is technically true, but he's responsible for hurting Mrs. Capps and for whatever happened to the bodyguards out front."

A paramedic paused in front of Kimberly, then turned to one of the police officers. "Order a second ambulance."

Kimberly grabbed Alex's arm. "No, I don't want to go."

"Look, ma'am, with Mrs. Capps unconscious, it's your only option. If we didn't have so many calls tonight, we could stay here while you delivered the placenta and maybe get Mrs. Capps's daughter out here, but that isn't possible."

"You know her?"

"Delivered me twenty-three years ago. We will take good care of both of you," the paramedic said, then wrapped a blanket around Kimberly's shoulders.

Alex smoothed her hair. "I won't leave you."

"I know," she said as the lights blinked twice, then came on.

ALEX STAYED IN KIMBERLY'S HOSPITAL room for the next thirty-six hours as the chaos subsided. He only left a few times to visit Mrs. Capps, who'd required surgery on a broken hip, and to answer questions. The envelope Elle had retrieved held most of the answers. Thompson Investments had been laundering money for a drug cartel for over a decade—a fact Jeremy hadn't learned until after he'd been transferred to the West Coast. Agent Danes was on the cartel's payroll and ordered the hits on his former partner and Jeremy. Agent Garcia regained consciousness and testified how Danes had tried to kill her when she'd uncovered the truth. They had rounded up the other accomplices in the smaller branch post office and low budget motel in Shipshewana.

He tried to explain this to Kimberly in a reasonable manner, but Kimberly held up a hand. "Bottom line—Jeremy was trying to do the right thing but was working with an agent who also worked for the cartel and that's why he was killed?"

"Yes."

"So am I still in danger?" Kimberly rocked her baby.

"No. The information the cartel wanted is now in the hands of the FBI, and numerous arrests have been made. Jeremy is a hero."

Tears welled up in Kimberly's eyes. "Can I have some time alone?"

Alex sat outside her room for hours and was never invited back in.

Kimberly held her pen above the standard form. Her son needed a name. Over the last few weeks, she had toyed with Zander, but now that Jeremy was a hero, it seemed wrong to name her son after a man she would soon divorce. Alex hadn't returned to her room since she'd asked for time alone. And without her phone, she couldn't contact him even if she knew what to say.

A memory that had been buried with the hopes of a child soon after her first marriage surfaced. She and Jeremy had been surfing baby-name sites, laughing at the most ridiculous names they could come up with. Xzatvian had been the clear winner.

Jeremy rubbed her still-flat tummy. "I like Clay. It was my grandpa's name. Clay Warner. Probably the best man I ever knew. He used to tell me stories about my mom and take me fishing."

Kimberly reached for the baby snuggled against her. "What do you think, Clay?"

Her little son opened his mouth in search of nourishment. Kimberly quickly wrote "Clay" on the line. The harder part was the last name. As much as she despised her father-in-law, his last name was Jeremy's last name. She finished the paperwork and signed her name.

"Okay, Clay Warner Thompson. Time to eat."

Alex wandered through the house, the little pieces of Kimberly's life scattered about the place causing his heart to ache. A hairband on the coffee table, a burp cloth on the back of the chair, sandals on the library floor. He found her in the loft, lying on a beanbag and staring at the skylight. Clay lay next to her.

"I came to say goodbye. And to give Clay this." He reached behind him for the brown-paper-wrapped quilt.

She turned from the window and took the package. "Goodbye?"

"Your life is no longer in danger. My job is done." *Give me permission to stay.*

"Oh. I guess you're right." Kimberly set the package near her feet.

"Do you know where you will go?" Alex settled into the other beanbag.

"I need to go to California. The authorities are letting me into the house to collect a few personal items before they auction everything off."

"Then what?"

"Candace has offered me a month-to-month lease if I want to stay here. I took one month so far. I hired a charter flight so I don't have to fly commercial with Clay." She brushed a finger across her son's brow. "I'd rather not expose him to a gazillion airport germs."

"Wise mama. May I see you when you get back?"

Kimberly bit her lip and looked up at the skylight again. "Alex, I wish ... I'm sorry. No. I wish—"

The answer didn't surprise him. They'd had this conversation too often. "If you ever need me—"

"I know. I trust you like I've never trusted anyone, especially a bodyguard. But a single mom is where I need to be. I wish I could give you hope there might be a someday. You deserve better. You deserve a real marriage. My lawyer should get things sorted out soon."

Alex swallowed the lump in his throat and reached over to touch the downy hair on Clay's head. It was as close as he dared get to touching her, to pulling her into his arms and convincing her she was wrong. Getting Lover's Loft to do its magic. He looked from the baby's newborn-blue eyes to Kimberly's brown ones. Her pupils widened. Perhaps she was thinking of magic too? She looked away, focusing her attention on Clay. "Goodbye, Alex."

He watched her for a moment more before leaving. He paused on the stairs. "I love you."

AGENT GREEN FOLLOWED KIMBERLY THROUGH her old house, cataloging the items Kimberly wanted to keep.

"This lace tablecloth was my grandmother's."

The agent nodded at a worker, who added the cloth to the growing pile of items they were letting Kimberly keep.

"This painting was a birthday gift from my friend Candace."

"What's it worth?"

"I don't know. I've never had it appraised."

The painting stayed on the wall.

"These books are mine. They are all signed to me."

The agent opened the front cover of the nearest one. "This is a first-edition Leigh Benz, signed and dated on release day. You have a full collection of first copies. The collection is valued at over $50,000. Leigh Benz rarely signs her work."

"Really? I had no clue the set was worth that much," Kimberly muttered more to herself than the agent.

"*The Caterpillar's Heart* is signed to your husband, not you. In fact, none are signed to you."

"No, but *Caterpillar's Special Day* is signed to 'Dearest Child,' which makes it Clay's book."

"I'll put these down, but I doubt you'll get them. They are too valuable. Someone paid a pretty penny for them. Maybe if you have receipts."

Kimberly looked at the agent. Where had he been the last two months? "They didn't cost a penny. They were complimentary author copies."

The agent shook his head. "So no receipts?"

"Why would I need a receipt?"

"To prove they didn't come from your husband's money."

Kimberly set the book down and looked the agent in the eye. "You're aware Leigh Benz is a pseudonym, right? In fact, it is my pseudonym. I didn't pay for the books because I wrote and illustrated them."

The agent's eyes grew wide. "No kidding?"

"How long have you been working on this case? If you don't believe me, call Agent Garcia. I know she just got out of the hospital, so she will only be slightly annoyed."

"They assigned me to this case earlier this week to assess the contents of the house. I was informed nothing was to be sold until you claimed your property. But I need proof that the valuable stuff is yours."

"Then right now I am claiming I am Leigh Benz, a fact your superiors will verify. It is my signature in these books, and they are mine. They have nothing to do with the Thompson estate, including the one I signed for my husband. It may be the only thing Clay inherits. Also, the Candace Wilson Ogilvie painting will go with me, or I will call her and get her lawyer involved."

The agent swallowed.

"Now, can we continue with this? I don't want to be here any more than you do." Kimberly desperately wanted to be cuddling Clay.

"Let's continue with the contents of the next room." Kimberly followed the agent around the corner into her studio.

She gasped at the damage. Her father-in-law had torn through every cabinet and desk in her studio. No wonder he had discovered her identity. There were a handful of preliminary sketches in the secret drawers, but her sketchbooks and finished work were safe in a climate-controlled storage vault with her manager. "If there is anything still useable in this room, it's mine. I know your directions are not to touch, but there were some hidden items I would like to check for. May I?" Kimberly kicked the bottom of the large cabinet, not waiting for an answer. It swung out two inches. Empty. The sketches inside hadn't been for her books. They'd been part of her journal, including sketches of her unborn baby, of the view from the stateroom on their cruise, and of Jeremy laughing. "Have any sketches turned up at the other estate or the office?"

"I don't know, ma'am."

"I would like to look at the artwork or sketches found at any of the Thompson holdings. As you noted with the books, they are valuable, but some are more valuable to me than they would be to any collectors."

"I'll see what I can do about that. Most of the other estate has been cleared for auction."

"Has the auction taken place yet?"

"No, it has to wait until after the trial."

"Then I want to see any drawings, paintings, or sketches. And the Monet in the master bedroom is a fake."

"Yes, I noticed."

Kimberly checked her watch. It was almost time to feed Clay. "Every paintbrush, canvas, paint, pencil, and what all from this room, other than the broken furniture. Also, the stained-glass window. It was a wedding present."

"But that's a Tessa Cavanagh!" This agent knew his stuff.

"Tessa Doyle. She gave it to me before she got married. And yes, she was my roommate." Kimberly turned to talk to Alex, then remembered he wasn't there. "Can we be finished now?"

"You haven't looked upstairs. Your clothing."

"I am assuming you have been through it all and cataloged it."

"That is my job."

She pictured him counting her underthings. "I don't need any of it. Donate it to a shelter or something."

"No jewelry?"

"I already have my mother's wedding ring and my grandmother's earrings. I can't think of a single other thing I want."

"Well then, Mrs. Thomp—"

"Mrs. Ha—I mean Benoit." She'd gotten used to Hastings, but it wasn't her right to use the name.

"Yes, we will inventory this and ship it to you."

"May I take the books and tablecloth now?" She hoped the question sounded more like a command.

"I'll clear that with my supervisor." The agent left her alone.

Kimberly spun in a slow circle, taking in the building she used to call home one last time. *Home.* The word conjured a feeling she no longer associated with California. A picture of Alex holding Clay came to mind. If only he could be her home.

They hadn't spoken since Clay was three days old. If he'd waited a week…

Kimberly left the house with too many regrets following her.

This date was going south fast. Alex tapped his phone three times. In seconds, a call came in from dispatch. Alex looked at the screen and gave the blonde next to him an apologetic smile. "I need to take this call. It's work."

"Oh, work. That is so brave." The woman batted her eyes and tried to squeeze his bicep again.

Alex put the phone to his ear and, pointing outside the little café, excused himself from their table.

"Good evening, Mr. Alexander. Can I help you?" asked Elle's cheery voice.

"Elle, you are working dispatch?"

"Alan wants me learning everything as long as I'm not in the field. What did you need?"

"You called. That was all I needed."

"Oh, the dating-app date is tonight, isn't it? That bad? Do you need to talk longer?"

Alex checked over his shoulder to see his date watching him intently. "Another minute, please."

"Oh, I have another call. Can I put you on hold?"

The music—Johnny Lee's "Looking for Love" chorus—started playing before he could answer. The hold music should have been classical. Subtlety wasn't Elle's strong point. She'd already pointed out he shouldn't be going on this date at all since he was still a married man. Alex ended the call and returned to the table.

"Do you need to go? We can reschedule." The blonde bounced in her seat.

"Look, it was nice to meet you, but I don't think we should set up a second date."

Her face fell.

"You're a real nice person, but my last relationship is still too much on my mind. Thanks for meeting me for dessert. I hope you have a good week." Alex left five dollars on the table as a tip, glad he'd paid for their desserts at the counter so there would be no awkward waiting.

"It was nice to meet you, Alex. Call me once your heart is healed."

Her hair would be gray by then.

Alex drove to the office, hoping there would be something to do. Anything but go back to his condo and dream of the little family he didn't have.

Kimberly turned the sketch upside down and looked at it again. Something was wrong. She checked the windows of the Art House studio. The lighting was good.

Clay cooed from the bassinet next to her. The Amish quilt Alex had given her curled around her son like a soft hug.

"What do you think? Did Mommy make a mistake?"

Another coo accompanied by a puckered face.

"A kissy face?"

Clay opened his mouth and let out a wail.

"Oh, a Mommy-I-need-to-be-picked-up-and-held face." Kimberly lifted him and balanced him against her shoulder. "I think I need to be held too." And there was only one person in the world she wanted to fill that position.

OGILVIE TOWER ROSE HIGH OVERHEAD. Kimberly checked her baby sling to make sure Clay's head was supported. The lobby clock informed her they were five minutes early. She nodded at the security guard as he checked her diaper bag before nodding her through to the bank of elevators.

Elle sat at the reception desk. "Good morning, Kimberly. Mr. Alexander will be out in a minute. Do you want to sit in the lobby or back in the conference room?"

"May I sit in the conference room?" If his reaction to seeing her in the office was negative, she didn't want any witnesses. She followed Elle past several cubicles to a small room.

"Would you like water? Soda?"

"May I have some water, please?" Was it better to face the door or not? Clay mewed in his sleep. Kimberly patted him and chose the chair farthest from the door, facing it.

Elle returned with two bottles of water and leaned in close. "Don't worry. Just smile. Everything will be great." On her way out, Elle shut the door.

Kimberly kissed the top of Clay's head. "Mommy is doing the right thing, right?"

The jiggle of the doorknob gave her a millisecond to take a deep breath.

Alex took a step into the room and froze. "Kimberly?"

"Hi, Alex."

"Why are you here?"

"I need a bodyguard." Her voice was unsteady.

He closed the door. "Why?"

Kimberly rubbed Clay's back, gleaning strength from her little one. "My heart is in danger of breaking, and I'm hoping he will help guard it."

He took a step closer. "Is there a particular bodyguard you have in mind?"

"I think there is only one who can adequately do the job."

"Just adequately? We strive for much better than adequately." He stood close enough that Kimberly could smell the spice of his aftershave.

She craned her neck to look up at him. He pulled out the chair next to her and slowly lowered himself into it. "How long do you need this bodyguard's services?"

"Fifty or sixty years at a minimum?" Her voice squeaked.

"That long?"

"Longer—if you can manage it. I don't think I have enough money to pay you what you're worth ..." Kimberly took a deep breath to make sure her next words came out right. "But I can pay you with all the love in my heart."

"You didn't answer my first question. Who do you want?"

"You. I want you. I love you. I think I have for a while. I just didn't know it." Great. She was tearing up.

Alex leaned forward over Clay and touched his lips to hers, then pulled back. "I'll take the job on one condition."

"Condition?"

"You pay me one kiss every day for the rest of your life."

"Just one?" She should have brought the car carrier. Kissing over Clay's head was more awkward than she could have imagined.

"I accept tips." Alex smiled one of his heart-melting smiles.
"When can you start?"

Alex stood and offered her his hand. "How about now?"

Taking his hand, she stood, and Alex wrapped both Kimberly and Clay in his embrace. Kissing with a baby in between them was much easier when standing. Alex ended the kiss and rested his head on hers. "I accept the job. I don't have a contract, but I have a ring. Will that work?"

"A ring? When did you get a ring?"

"The day after Mother's Day. It just never seemed like the right time to give it to you. It's in my truck."

"Before you go get it, I do have a contract of sorts. And if neither of us signs it and we don't file it, we will still be married." Kimberly pulled his face down to meet his lips again.

"I have a paper shredder. I think we should shred your contract immediately."

"Agreed. Do you mind terribly if we arrange a renewal-of-our-vows ceremony? I'd like to wear makeup and look you in the eye and know I mean every word."

"Amish dress?"

"No way."

"Deal." Alex pulled her into another kiss, and Clay squawked. Alex planted a kiss on his head. "And what about this one?"

"I think he should grow up with your name and calling you Dad. Will you adopt him?"

"In a heartbeat."

Kimberly rubbed Clay's back. "When he is old enough to understand, I'll explain how wise Jeremy was, and he can be proud of both dads."

"And of his clever mother." Alex leaned in for another kiss before he asked for the rest of the day off.

Epilogue

Kimberly set the red candles in the candle holders and smoothed her grandmother's lace tablecloth, then fussed with the bow on Alex's gift—Leigh Benz's latest book about a friendship between Zander the bear and Kim the cardinal. His version was the kind of love story that wasn't kid friendly.

Her phone buzzed. The Hastings Security app came in handy for knowing when Alex was pulling into the garage. Out of habit, she looked around for Clay to see what trouble the eighteen-month-old was into, and then she remembered tonight's chaos would be for Grandma Hastings to deal with. The brave woman was hosting a sleepover for all the grandchildren other than the triplets. She was the bravest mother-in-law in the world. Or maybe father-in-law, as Melanie had recruited Jethro to be her number-one helper.

Kimberly waited in the dining room, the door between the garage and kitchen closed. Alex came in, took one look at the table set with her fine china, and wrapped her in a hug, nuzzling her neck. "Did I miss something? Valentine's Day isn't until Sunday, right?"

"You didn't miss anything. Your brave parents are having a toddler sleepover tonight."

"So Clay is gone all night?" Alex placed a line of kisses along her jaw.

"Mmm-hmm."

"So he won't crawl into our bed at four in the morning?" He moved to her favorite spot behind her ear.

"No. We will be all alone."

Alex pulled back. "It sounds like Mom and Dad want more grandkids."

"Good thing. They should have one around Labor Day."

"What!"

"Congratulations, Dad."

Alex let out a whoop as he spun Kimberly in a circle.

"You're sure?"

"Yes. I'm only about six weeks, but I am doing well."

"Does this have anything to do with your trip to Art House yesterday and the loaf of friendship bread?"

"Mrs. Capps says hello." Kimberly pushed him toward a chair. "We can kiss more after I eat."

"Promise?"

"Yes. I still owe you your daily tip."

acknowledgements

THANKS TO CAMI WHO SPENDS many morning walks listening to me talk about all of the problems of my imaginary friends. To the real Barbra Samuels and Debbie Capps whose names appear in this book as a reward for supporting a great cause. I love you both! Thanks for letting me use your names.

As always thanks to Tammy and Nanette who are so willing to help make all my projects better and to read for all my mistakes. I would never make it through a day without Sally and Cindy whose advice keeps me going. Thank you wonderful ladies.

Michele at Eschler Editing does the best edits; any mistakes left in this book are not her fault. Nor are my excellent proofreaders to be blamed. Thank you ladies and gents!

My family, for sharing their home with the fictional characters who often got fed better than they did. And my husband who encourages me every crazy step of the way and puts up with all my messy spreadsheets.

And to my Father in Heaven for putting these wonderful people, and any I may have forgotten to mention, in my life. I am grateful for every experience and blessing I have been granted.

about the author

Lorin Grace was born in Colorado and has been moving around the country ever since, living in eight states and several imaginary worlds. She graduated from Brigham Young University with a degree in Graphic Design.

Currently she lives in northern Utah with her husband, four children, and a dog who is insanely jealous of her laptop. When not writing, Lorin enjoys creating graphics, visiting historical sites, museums, and reading.

Lorin is an active member of the League of Utah Writers and was awarded Honorable Mention in their 2016 creative writing contest short romance story category. Her debut novel, *Waking Lucy,* was awarded a 2017 Recommended Read award in the LUW Published book contest. In 2018 Mending Fences with the Billionaire, also received a Recommended Read award.

You can learn more about her, and sign up for her writers club at loringrace.com or at Facebook: LorinGraceWriter